Annie Flint

The Christmas Stocking

a choice collection of charming stories

Annie Flint

The Christmas Stocking
a choice collection of charming stories

ISBN/EAN: 9783337382360

Printed in Europe, USA, Canada, Australia, Japan

Cover: Foto ©Andreas Hilbeck / pixelio.de

More available books at **www.hansebooks.com**

Annie Flint

The Christmas Stocking
a choice collection of charming stories

ISBN/EAN: 9783337382360

Printed in Europe, USA, Canada, Australia, Japan

Cover: Foto ©Andreas Hilbeck / pixelio.de

More available books at **www.hansebooks.com**

THE

CHRISTMAS STOCKING,

BY COUSIN VIRGINIA.

A CHOICE
COLLECTION OF CHARMING STORIES.

———

NEW YORK:

HURST & CO., PUBLISHERS,

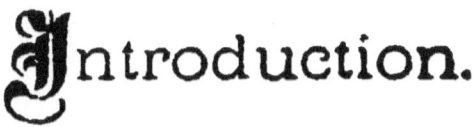ntroduction.

CHRISTMAS EVE had come and the children were at last asleep, dreaming of the pleasures in store for them on the morrow, while I sat by the fire completing a soft crimson shawl—my gift to mother.

The gay-colored worsted slipped through my fingers scarcely less rapidly than my thoughts flitted from one subject to another—thoughts of the home circle, shielded by walls of love from rough contact with the outer world; of the poor to whom the Christmas light would bring no ray of warmth or hope, perhaps; and the peaceful country farm-houses, where abundance of spicy mince-pies and frosted cakes awaited keen young appetites.

The clock struck twelve, in soft silvery chimes, as I snipped the worsted fringe and folded the shawl over mother's armchair, where she would notice it in the morning; then I drew aside the curtain to look out upon the night. The snow had ceased falling, and now lay in feathery drifts on the silent city, like a pure white veil, crisply defined on the eaves, dimpled in softer masses over the roofs, and tracing graceful patterns among the dark trees of the square, where a fountain glittered in crystal pendants of ice, while the stars in the clear sky above had the steely brilliancy of extreme cold.

"A pleasant night for Santa-Claus to ramble abroad," I said, aloud.

"Here I am, my dear," replied a merry voice by the hearth; and sure enough, there stood the little man, as beamingly good-natured and rosy as he has always been described.

"Five stockings to fill," he continued, searching his capacious pockets. "Let me see. A sugar doll or so, to begin with; and a tin trumpet never comes amiss. Which is yours?"

"I am too old to hang up my stocking," I laughed.

"Not too old to receive one, at al' events," and Santa-Claus actually tossed a little silk stocking into my lap, before he scrambled up chimney again to pursue his journey.

My stocking contained stories, I discovered when I pened it, and here they are.

CONTENTS.

The Christmas Stocking.

Harry May.

OWN on the Penobscot, before the broad expanse of bay narrows into the smaller boundary of river, stands a sleepy little town; but we must not tell the name, because it is not at all sleepy and dull to the people who call it "home," probably, and Harry May certainly never found it so.

The range of houses extends from the water's edge up the sloping hill-side, each one very trim and neat, and on the summit stands the large old church. or "meeting-house," the weather-stained roof and narrow windows visible for miles around. harry had so much to do, he never grew dull in this quiet nook of a place. He could paddle out in the mud after clam-shells at low tide, or catch an unfortunate crab, left stranded on the sand ; and there cannot be better fun than these pursuits, unless it be scrambling about on some vessel, all tar and fresh paint, and pretending to be captain of the craft.

Sometimes the boy paused to watch the sun set over the harbor, mellowing the outline of the distant hills with a softened haze mantle, cresting the clear waves with rose and blue tints, where the natty little revenue cutter rode at anchor, the brass cannon on the deck flashing in the waning light, and the fishing-boats glided out for a night's work among the haddock of the bay, while the clouds floated lazily in the blue sky above.

The summer only smiled briefly in this cold region, but the winter brought no fears to Harry; there was sliding down hill to be done, skating, perhaps a sleigh-ride or two with Uncle James, wrapped up to the ears in furs; no end of snow-balling among the boys, and the building of snow-men.

Harry lived on the outskirts of the town, in a low, old-fashioned house, where he had a little chamber over the kitchen all to himself—that was quite like a man, for he was the only child in the household.

His father was a sea-captain, and it was a long, long time since any tidings of the absent sailor had reached the anxious hearts at home, so that the mother grew pale and careworn with weary watching, and the townspeople began to say among themselves that the "Rebecca" would never come back again.

Harry remembered the day very well when the bark, built of the timber hewn in the interior by the stalwart lumbermen—his father's own vessel—sailed for California on the long, stormy voyage round Cape Horn, and how proud he felt to see the sails fill to the breeze, as she swept through the waters gracefully and disappeared.

The careless boy would often forget all about the sorrow weighing upon the household, when he was at play with his schoolmates, until he returned home to find grandfather searching the newspaper files for tidings of the lost vessel, while his mother and Aunt Jane sat at their work.

"When I am a grown man," thought Harry, lying in his bed at night, looking out at the bright stars through the small window, "I shall build a ship and go after father. Perhaps he's living on some little island, where they drink water out of shells, and find what they want to eat, like the Swiss family Robinson."

Perhaps it was just as well he should not realize that his father might be resting beneath the cruel waters, away down where the corals grow and silken tangles of sea-weed wave; where the medusæ float in the darkness of night, like globes of pale-green fire, and strange forms flash along, mere ribbons of gleaming, silvery foam—so often the sailor's grave.

Grandfather had been the village postmaster for years, and he also was a farmer to a small extent; he owned several acres of land, and a comfortable barn, the favorite resort of a colony of swallows, where the cow and the old horse lived, while the fowls came and went at their own pleasure. Grandfather was not a terrible old gentleman in the least, afraid of a trifle of noise, such as the sound of Harry's drum, which Aunt Jane declared set her very teeth on edge, and always bade him go out-doors and give the pigs a military tattoo.

Yes, it was different with Aunt Jane; she was very particular in her ways, and always wanted the parlor blinds drawn close to keep out the flies, so that the place smelled of varnish and damp. As for the best spare chamber, no visitor was ever good enough to occupy the state bedstead, with the fresh muslin curtains starched stiff and ornamented with bows of gay-colored ribbons, except a clergyman. Aunt Jane could make the lightest bread, the crispest cakes, and the most delicious sweetmeats that ever were tasted by any small boy, yet unfortunately she never thought Harry should eat the latter dainties, such things were not good for young stomachs. Still, he received his full share, after all, from mother; and often grandfather, with a merry wink and nod, would slip some delicacy into the little man's pocket when Aunt Jane was not looking, for like all amiable people he dreaded a scolding, and his daughter was not an amiable woman, although she tried to do her duty in the world.

Oh, these maiden aunts, how they trample down the air-castles of infant imagination, and nag youthful tempers over the hand-washing and pinafore strings of life !

When Harry was nine years old he had a desperately dangerous adventure, which made him a hero among his companions for months afterward. The children never tired of the history, the boys telling boastfully what they would have done, had they been in Harry's place ; while the little girls, less courageous by nature, contented themselves with opening their eyes very wide and listening.

Early in the spring the church was opened one evening for a service. It was a very unusual event, as the upper school-room in the academy building generally served for prayer-meetings, but. now a missionary had come to visit the minister, who had lived in India for years, and he was to lecture upon his distant home on the Ganges ; so the old sexton trimmed the oil-lamps, and the church presented a very fine appearance, rays of light blinking through all the windows like so many bright eyes.

What should our small friend Harry do but climb the hill to peep in where the sexton was pulling the bell-rope to warn the community that it was half-past seven o'clock. Harry had a great respect for the sexton; it always seemed to the child that the church could no more do without him than the minister himself, or the singers.

The boy stood looking in the door a moment, then obeying a sudden impulse, darted up-stairs into the side gallery. There he sat peering at the people as they came in, his curly head and bright eyes just on a level with the gallery railing. It was capital fun to look down, without being seen.

There sat grandfather and mother; beyond was Deacon Wright, who wore such a queer brown wig, and old Mrs. Scudder, whose double chins Harry had tried to count many a time.

The lady at the organ played; Susan Gray, with the pink bonnet-strings sang in the choir; and then after a time the missionary began to speak.

At first Harry looked at the missionary, but what he said was not very interesting; he could point out Bombay on the map, with his chubby forefinger, if the teacher told him to do so: further than that, he had not thought half as much about the subject as the owning of a new top.

He yawned, stretched himself out upon the seat in a comfortable position so that he could look up at the church ceiling, until the missionary's voice sounded drowsily afar off, and Harry's eyes closed.

He dreamed he stood upon the ice, and the surface was so smoothly polished, like a mirror, that
he slipped repeatedly, while other children glided
past him swiftly as birds, upon flashing skates. He
wished for skates too, and no sooner had he felt
the desire than one of the children brought a pair to
him, which he gladly strapped upon his feet, and
started with the rest.

There never was such skating. The stranger-child,
who had brought the skates, joined hands with
Harry, and they flew along past the snow-clad hills,
villages, and cities extending roof beyond roof, such
as the boy had never before seen ; and once they
paused to write their names upon the ice with the
sharp steel edge of their skates—Harry May could
be distinctly read.

All at once they slid into a green wood, where
the lofty branches interlaced overhead so that only
stray glints of sunshine could penetrate the shady
avenues, where the wind rustled over the nodding
wild-flowers on mossy banks, and the squirrels
nibbled their nuts undisturbed.

An arbor opened before them, the walls of which
were living plants entwined so as to support an airy
dome of fragrant roses ; and here sat a funny little
old woman in a red cap and ruffled petticoat, such
as fairies wear, with a reading-desk before her, on
which was placed a large book.

She smiled a good-day to the children, gave them

each a stick of candy, and then opened her great
picture-book for their amusement.

"What do you see?" she asked.

It was a large toy-shop, stocked with everything
delightful.   Hobby-horses pranced, locomotives
whistled along miniature railway-tracks, guns were
fired by groups of stiff soldiers, pasteboard castles
had flags floating from the turrets, and the whole
place was festooned with dolls, pretty dolls, ugly
dolls, crying and talking dolls, some of them dangling by one foot, others crowded together in tiers,
so that they could not move as much as a kid
finger.

"What do you see now?" inquired Dame Imagination, for that was her name, and Harry considered it a very long one indeed.

Vast prairies spread out before the gaze, with a
rugged outline of mountains looming against the
distant horizon, and a band of hunters were travel-
ling cautiously along in search of buffalo, to replenish
their stock of provisions.   The hunters wore gay
scarfs and moccasins, and so brown had their faces
become from exposure in the rough life they led,
that one could scarcely distinguish them from the
Indian guides.

Now they approached the herd, and the Indians,
mounted on swift horses, dashed fearlessly among
the savage animals, launching their arrows with un-
erring aim, while the buffalo, bellowing wrathfully,

fled over the plain, occasionally turning to attack their pursuers.

"Those are the Rocky Mountains!" exclaimed Harry, proud of his geography.

"What comes next?" pursued the old dame, turning another leaf and fixing her eyes upon the children.

A Chinese temple gorgeously painted and richly gilt, where stood statues of heathen gods, half concealed by drooping banners, and heavily embroidered draperies of yellow—the sacred color.

Yes, it was splendid, one could even smell the fragrance of aromatic perfumes lingering in the atmosphere, and the wax tapers twinkled brightly before the altar of the idols, stiffly erect, with narrow Chinese eyes, and hair braided in long tails. The priest burned prayers and leaves of gold paper before the shrine : that answered quite as well as reciting them, it was considered.

What the next picture of this book of fancy would have revealed Harry never knew, for at that moment he rolled off from the narrow seat upon the floor.

Everything was very dark and still. For some time the truth did not dawn upon the poor little man—that the people had all gone home, and he was left alone in the terrible place.

Harry did not feel in the least brave ; on the contrary, he was so terrified that the blood ran chill in his veins, and he would have shrieked aloud had he dared.

Even grown people sometimes have a nervous fear of the dark, and any child would have immediately begun to fancy bogeys and hobgoblins forming or shifting about among the dense shadows, prepared to pounce upon the little wanderer, so far away from mother—just as Harry did.

He stumbled along the gallery, whimpering quietly to himself, in search of the door, hurting himself against the seats, and once tumbling over a footstool with a crash. Oh dear, where was the door?—not where it had been when he came in, surely. No, the door had not changed its place, but Harry had guided himself along the wall to the wrong end of the gallery, by the pulpit, in his bewilderment. To add to his dismay, the moon peeped through the drifting cloud-masses, shedding a pale, uncertain light through the blinds, here and there serving to outline the gloom into fresh forms of terror before Harry's wide-opened eyes.

We must leave him for a short space of time, while we see what was happening at home.

When grandfather came home from meeting at nine o'clock, Aunt Jane sat by the bright kitchen fire knitting. She had only just returned from a visit to the next neighbor, who was suffering from rheumatism, and the house had been left open during her absence, as there was little danger of burglars.

"Has Harry gone to bed?" inquired the mother.

"I forgot him entirely," replied Aunt Jane, looking up from her work.

"Perhaps he is up stairs," said Mrs. May.

She went to his little chamber, where the bed was undisturbed by the usually weary young occupant, and profound silence answered her, when she called his name. The barn was visited, to the surprise of the sleepy cow, and every nook of the premises, until the mother became seriously alarmed.

"He is still at play, perhaps," suggested Aunt Jane, trying to reassure her.

"But it is so late," urged Mrs. May.

"True," assented her sister thoughtfully. "We will go out and find him."

At the moment they started Master Harry was curled up like a kitten in the gallery, dreaming of the wonderful picture-book.

They hurried along, inquiring at several places where the boy had playmates, only to find that all the little ones were safely asleep: then they pursued their way to Mr. Clarke's store, as it was a favorite resort—a kind of country club-room, where men lounged about on barrels and the counter, after the labors of the day, to hear the latest news.

No person had seen Harry since dark.

Kind Mr. Clarke, fearing that something was amiss, led Mrs. May into his own house next door, and requested her to remain there while he made a thorough search for the lost child.

Soon the whole town heard the tidings, for it was not often that anything occurred to disturb the stillness of night. Heads were thrust forth from windows, questions were asked; then fathers came forth to join the party, armed with lanterns; and Mr. Clarke inquired at every house for Harry.

Finally it was proposed they should search along the shore : perhaps he had drifted off into the harbor in a boat ; perhaps he was asleep in the steamboat baggage-shed. They thought of everything that could happen to a small boy, except getting locked into the church.

They were fully a half-hour exploring the beach, but at length they were compelled to retrace their steps without a clew of any sort.

Mrs. May met them at the gate with pale face and trembling frame ; even Aunt Jane's countenance began to express grave concern.

"We shall find him, yet," said Mr. Clarke soothingly ; "the little scamp may be hiding somewhere."

Nobody believed this to be true, not even the good man himself; still, he felt that something must be said to comfort the poor mother. Fortunately the old sexton came plodding along to the store for some tea, and as he lived on the other side of the town he had not yet heard the alarm.

'Have you seen Harry?" cried Aunt Jane, despairingly.

The sexton paused to think.

"Why, some little boy watched me ring the bell."

"Bless us!" interposed Aunt Jane, who was very quick to arrive at a conclusion. "He must be in the meeting-house, after all," and she started toward the church, pushing back her hood in her excitement.

Master Harry was still alive, and had found his way down stairs to the front door at last, with much difficulty. He no sooner heard voices approaching than he gained sufficient courage to scream and kick against the portal with his stout little boots. The sexton turned the key and the small figure stood revealed in the light of the lanterns.

Mother and Aunt Jane immediately smothered him with caresses, the latter bestowing more kisses in her joy and gratitude than she had ever given before in his life.

The neighbors laughed over the adventure, as they dispersed in different directions, while mother asked a dozen questions of Harry, who could only reply in sobs and tears.

How pleasant it was to see grandpa's face again, which was enough, in its placid beauty, to drive away all the bugbears out of a young brain!

How delightful to have mother smooth the pillow and tuck in the blankets; even Aunt Jane bringing a bowl of milk porridge, her favorite remedy for all ills of the flesh !—not that Harry needed it in the least, but only as a polite attention on her part. Then to gradually fall asleep, so snug and safe, and forget all about the dreary darkness of the grim church !

This experience of our small friend kept every child awake on Sunday for any length of time. If one of them felt disposed to doze, after watching the flies buzz on the window-pane, or counting the brass nails in the pulpit, Harry's mournful story was remembered, and the little one dreaded being left in the same way, although it was broad day-light.

Two months passed away and the summer came once more, not indeed with the rich abundance of luxuriant foliage and delicious fruits of warmer latitudes, but to tinge sea and sky a softer blue, and clothe the river-banks with a mantle of tender green.

Imagine Harry's delight when his mother received a letter one morning, inviting her to visit an old friend beyond Bangor. Harry was included in the invitation, and he could do nothing but caper about joyfully when she consented to go after Aunt Jane had not only urged her doing so, but commenced to pack such articles as were needed for the journey.

The ever-present weight of suspense and anxiety which Mrs. May had borne for so long, since any tidings from her absent husband had entirely ceased, was gradually affecting her health, and it was considered desirable she should have a change of scene for a time at least.

Harry had once been on the steamboat when he was a little baby, still he did not remember that occasion very clearly, so he now looked forward with great interest to the moment when the boat should approach to take *him* on board ; an interest which he felt sure every one else shared with himself.

He carried a luncheon-basket well provisioned, his mother a shawl, and thus equipped they walked to the wharf, after a shrill whistle had announced the approach of the steamer around the point, and the distant pulsations of her paddle-wheels, beating the water into frothing tracks of foam, grew more and more distinct, until a surging movement brought her alongside of the pier.

"Going away, Harry?" inquired Mr. Thornton, the minister, who was watching the boat's progress.

It seemed very grand to be able to answer that he was, and, after bidding grandpa good-bye, step upon the plank which led to the upper deck ; then have the wheels revolve again, the steamer swing slowly round to resume her voyage, and the town gradually fade into the distance, until a projecting hill concealed it entirely from view.

At first Harry felt shy among so many strangers. Most of the travellers looked jaded and pale, after spending the night on the rough coast, where they must have been sea-sick ; still, some of the number were yet fresh and bright.

Perched upon a stool on the deck, beside his mother, Harry watched the shores of the river, where villages clustered here and there, the church spires pointing to heaven, or some solitary farm-house nestled among the trees.

Presently another boy came out of the cabin, and stood by the bulwark. Harry regarded him with more interest than the scenery inspired.

" It looks just like ice-cream, don't it?" remarked the stranger-boy, pointing to the track of foam in the wake of the vessel.

Harry thought it did, although he had never tasted that delicacy but twice in his small life. To resemble ice-cream in flavor or appearance, is the highest tribute of praise a child can bestow on any-thing whatever.

" Are you in the Second Reader at school yet ?" pursued the stranger-boy ; "and can you do frac-tions ?"

" Yes," said Harry. " Where do you live ?"

" Just above Bangor, replied his new friend. " There comes my father ; is yours on board ?"

Harry was surprised to see his mother shake hands with the stranger-boy's father, who proved to be the brother of the friend they were to visit.

Frank Nichols was a year older than our hero, and he soon proposed that they should drink a glass

of water in the cabin, then ramble about in search
of amusement, while their parents talked together.
The children paused by the glass windows to watch
the machinery pump up and down ; they explored
the lower decks and passages, where a sickening
sea-smell pervaded everything ; and the negro waiters stepped along jauntily, beating gongs, or arranging long tables, where lights flickered feebly. They
returned safely, after a while, Harry wearing a very
long face, for a sudden breeze had blown his hat
overboard, and a stain of machine-oil had trickled
down upon the sleeve of his best jacket during his
explorations.

At last the spires and masts of Bangor were defined against the horizon, the steamboat blew a shrill
whistle as she entered her dock, and the passengers
landed.

Harry was dazzled with the large hotels, the streets
of gay shops, the handsome residences, and numbers
of people to be seen hastening along. What would
have been his sensations had he visited Boston, or
once beheld the brilliant beauty of New York at
night, when Madison Square, in the distance, resembles a crown of flashing jewels, with the illu-
minated hotels and club-houses for the solitaire
gems?

Mr. Nichols gave each of the boys a pretty rose-
colored balloon, which they held by a string as they
climbed to the top of the clumsy comfortable old

stage-coach for the remainder of the journey. They had not proceeded far when Harry's string parted, .nehow, and away went the balloon up into the air, in the most provoking way imaginable, sailing a.ong like a crimson bubble.

The river was in sight all the way, winding and foaming into rapids occasionally; no longer the broad stream on which the steamboats could float, but still affording means of transport for the lumber rafts to be guided down from the mills above to load vessels, and yielding delicious salmon.

Frank pointed out a mountain, across some ninety miles of level country, resting like a blue cloud in the distance, yet sharply defined in outline—Mount Katahdin, about which Mr. Winthrop wrote a beautiful book, although the boys knew nothing of that.

We must not linger to describe the warm greeting Mrs. May received from her friends in their pleasant home; how Frank promised to show Harry everything there was to be seen, the next morning; how the latter, together with his mother, occupied a fresh pretty chamber, with flowers painted upon the furniture; and a case of birds, their gay plumage carefully preserved, stood between the windows.

Nor can we dwell upon everything the two boys did, after Frank had nodded a good-morning to Harry across the street, before breakfast. They took walks together, they made boats out of chips to sail

on the water; they visited the mills, where the whirling clouds of dust and the rapid movements of the
machinery made them giddy; or they watched the
men walk fearlessly about upon the wet logs, far
out in the stream, which afforded them enough foot-
ing from long practice. Besides all these enjoy-
ments there was a picnic upon the banks of a tranquil
lake, and the children were allowed to wander
through the woods, discovering treasures at every
step;—now a silken tent in which a colony of caterpillars were snugly wrapped up on a leaf, to await a
change into perfect insects; now a little garden of
fully ripened wild strawberries, to be carefully gathered into a bouquet for mother, the fruit hanging
like scarlet tassels among the green stalks; now
some aromatic, glossy wintergreen leaves with fragile
white blossoms.

As the sun set and the breeze died away, how the
mosquitoes did sally forth in armies, ready to taste
fresh young cheeks and round soft arms!

A far more important event, however, was a visit
to the Penobscot tribe in their own homes on the
island at Old Town. Harry had seen some of the
Indians during their journeyings down the river,
where they sold the pretty basket-work, woven by
their skilful fingers; but he had a vague idea, gathered chiefly from the pictures in his school-books,
that some terrible chief, like King Philip, all war-
paint and feathers, still existed at the native settlement.

Two young men, with blue-black hair and dark bronze complexions, rowed the party across in a large bateau to their destination, where a cluster of houses surrounded the white church.

"There goes the chief, now," whispered Frank, as a graceful canoe darted swiftly through the water.

What a chief! only a stout man, wearing a broad felt hat and linen coat, a suitable costume for a railway journey.

Where were the wigwams, the tomahawks, the graceful maidens in embroidered moccasins, that the stories tell about? All gone, or at the best only found in the far West and Canada.

Instead of the wigwams, Harry found very dirty houses, into which the jealous inmates would scarcely allow the party to peep, for Indians do not like to be stared at, as objects of curiosity in their mode of living, any better than we should ourselves. Perhaps their numbers would not decrease so rapidly if they took some lessons in cleanliness from the neat New England housewives about them. Harry very well knew that the attic floor even, at home, under Aunt Jane's vigilant eye, would not soil a cambric handkerchief.

Instead of brandishing tomahawks, the men and boys lounged in the shade indolently, or built canoes in a leisurely fashion, working a little and resting a great deal ; and as for the graceful Indian maidens, represented by poets and artists as skipping lightly across foaming brooks, those that Harry saw were seated upon blankets, sewing red-print gowns of modern patterns, or weaving baskets, with their hair dressed in waterfalls, chewing spruce-gum.

Altogether, when he came away again the little boy concluded it would not be as much fun to become an Indian as he had before supposed, at times when Aunt Jane insisted upon his using the door-mat in order that the carpets should not receive an impress from muddy boots, or scolded him for pulling her favorite cat's tail.

Once indeed Harry had very nearly made up his mind to run away to the Indians, when Aunt Jane's cat was so angry at the sight of a puppy, a present to Harry, that she quite lost her appetite, and perched on the window-seat snarling, or fled to the roof, after a battle royal with the spirited little dog. The cat carried the day—the puppy was banished, and Harry felt miserable for about a week.

After the visit to Old Town the two boys decided it would be capital. sport to play Indian, and proceeded to execute the plan at once.

Mr. Nichols owned a canoe, but Frank had never managed it before ; still, he now determined to use it. Frank very well knew that his father would not have allowed him to use the canoe, and so he did not ask any permission. This was extremely naughty, for he did not pause to think that the reason why such a permission would not be granted was because it must be dangerous to manage the frail bark.

Harry seated himself carefully in the bottom of the swaying canoe, Frank took the paddle, and they crossed the stream where it was narrow.

"We will pretend to camp out, you know, he said, when they landed in the tall grass on the opposite bank, and drew the boat up after them. "If we only had some matches, now, we could make a gay fire."

"But there's no kettle," said practical Harry; "and besides, we might burn everything up."

The lack of matches, with which the young adventurers perhaps would have spread a vast conflagration, only made their active imaginations turn to other employments. They toiled over huge stones to make traps by braiding rushes and bushes together, for any wild animal that might chance to come that way, from an elephant to a wildcat; as it was, only an innocent cow walked into the snare. They hid behind rocks to shoot deer, with bow and arrows, and they performed the part of springing from ambush upon a party of travellers, with great courage, giving fearful war-whoops while they easily overpowered the imaginary pale-faces.

Mr. Nichols drove along the river-bank an hour later, returning home from a distance, and beheld the canoe rocking under the unsteady strokes of the paddle in Frank's inexperienced hand.

Mr. Nichols was a brave man, yet an involuntary exclamation of horror escaped from his lips, and his heart failed him, when he considered the frightful danger the children were threatened with at that moment. The canoe had drifted almost into the current above the fall, where a sluice-way had been built on one side for the use of the mills, when the river was too low to enable the rafts floating over the falls, and the slightest movement on the part of the boys might decide which course the boat would take; or they could easily overturn it and be thrown into the river, where they would speedily be carried to the brink, then dashed into the foaming abyss below, where sharp rocks stood revealed here and there like sharp teeth.

Mr. Nichols made his way down to the shore, where others were already hastening, aware of the peril. And now another fear beset him; some one would shout at the boys, and so further embarrass their movements sufficiently to carry them down the current.

An instant of intense suspense—the children fortunately benumbed and helpless with terror; then, guided by a divine hand, the canoe swerved round into the swift tide of the sluice-way.

Ben Derrick, the lumberman, had by this time climbed across rapidly to a drift of logs, and with the aid of a long pole, hooked the little boat and drew it gently up to the side of the sluice, while a large boat was pushed off from the shore to receive the three.

Courage returned to Frank and Harry when they once more trod upon firm ground; they only realized fully their danger when they saw the white anxious faces gathered about them.

This was certainly a more terrible adventure than that in the church.

"Father never scolded a bit," whispered Frank that night. "We won't try that again, though."

Harry was obliged to confess that he hoped he might never see a canoe again, especially after his mother told him how easily the boat would have upset and they been drowned, even before the other danger threatened.

The time of their visit had not fully expired when a letter came from Aunt Jane, requesting Mrs. May to return home. None of the family were ill, she wrote, and they had not received sad news from any source; still, if they were willing, she would like them to return

This letter naturally puzzled Mrs. May very much, yet she prepared to obey the summons at once, thinking that some accident must have befallen grandfather, as he was a very old man, and that the letter was worded in a guarded manner not to frighten her.

Harry, rather subdued by the canoe voyage, bade his friend Frank good-bye, and the two boys promised faithfully to write each other a long letter ; but they never did, they had so much else to think of as soon as they had separated.

The little boy felt that he had seen a great deal of the world, when he once more stood upon the deck of the steamer which was to convey him home again. He was not at all afraid to walk through the cabins by himself, to view the machinery, and show the tickets to the stewardess, as he had been before.

Down the sparkling river swiftly, until the familiar church-spire appeared in sight, and then the town clustered at the base of the hill.

A crowd of friends met them at the pier, all eager to shake hands and welcome Mrs. May home again, so cordially that one would imagine she had been absent two years instead of two weeks. She became quite confused by the pleasant greetings showered upon her : as she passed up the street beside Aunt Jane, people nodded from open windows and doors, and one little girl handed her a beautiful bouquet of fresh roses over the fence.

Mrs. May was a general favorite in the village ; still, she could not understand what occasioned the warmth of her greeting : as for foolish Harry, he trudged along in the pride of his heart, supposing that it was all because they had been gone away so long.

Aunt Jane appeared very gay also, and declared

that grandfather was quite we.l—there he stood at the gate now, waiting to receive them.

Harry's quick eye speedily detected another figure in the distance standing beside the old man, the slanting sun's rays gilding the snow-white head of age, and mellowing to a deeper bronze the sea-tanned face of vigorous manhood.

" It's father !" shouted the boy, throwing aside the luncheon-basket, and running toward him.

Yes, Captain May had returned home at last, when every one supposed he must be dead, and the townspeople rejoiced at the delightful surprise in store for Mrs. May.   He had been shipwrecked on the return voyage from China ; had passed days of almost incredible suffering in an open boat on the wide ocean, without water or food ; had been further detained by severe illness after his rescue by a passing ship.

Harry listened to the whole thrilling recital from his father's lips with eager attention.

That evening Harry was permitted to remain up later than usual, in honor of his father's return, and numerous friends flocked in, bringing every sort of delicacy, in the form of cake and pie, as refresh-ments for so large a company.

Harry wandered about among the throng, ate more doughnuts than was good for him, and finally fell fast asleep in a corner of the stairs, after the ex-citement of the day

Captain May lifted the small form in his arms tenderly, and carried him away to bed.

The moonlight shed a silvery radiance through the little window, tracing fitful patterns upon the floor, as father and mother stood together by Harry's bedside, thanking the good God for his mercy in uniting the family again, and praying that by their care the child's footsteps should be guided in the better path of life.

THE KINGDOM OF SHIMMER.

IN the kingdom of Shimmer peace had been at length restored, after many years of dissension ; for the Black Fairies would have it that the descendants of Prince Parsley should reign, whether male or female (there was no Salic law in fairy-land, you perceive), and the Blue Fairies declared for King Doddle, fighting under his banner so valiantly that the rival faction was finally subdued, and the sovereign allowed to ascend the throne.

The kingdom of Shimmer had suffered from the devastation of war ; the flowers had been trampled down by contending armies, and even the bees had been frightened away with the noise and hubbub of this dreadful internal conflict ; but now they could come back unmolested, for all Prince Parsley's family had been despatched with thorn-spike and wasp-sting weapons used by the tiny, cruel warriors.

The Black Fairies might sulk over their defeat in their homes, but it would do no good, and King Doddle only taxed them ten more violets as a tribute, to be paid yearly at the palace, for their ill-humor.

Among the Black Fairies, Dame Mustard had been a prominent rebel, encouraging her party to further mischief, when they would have owned King Doddle's sway before ; and for this unruly conduct she was shut up in an acorn prison, by the royal body-guard, and given only the bitter acorn crumbs to eat.

Of course Dame Mustard was not in a very good temper when she was released from so dreary a dungeon, and her ill-humor was only increased by finding that her pretty mansion in a gorgeous tulip had been taken possession of, during her absence, by a Blue Fairy, in high favor with the reigning house of Doddle.

"Never mind," she said, shaking her weazened little fist at the prosperous Blue Fairy ; "just wait a bit, and you will all hear from me again."

She then proceeded to an old stump of a tree, where she found a chamber of suitable size, and this she began to decorate in the most beautiful manner. She hung the walls with a tapestry of rose-leaves, the ceiling was draped with festoons of spider-silk, and the floor strewn with the golden pollen of flowers.

As for furniture, Dame Mustard did not care much about that, she merely heaped some dandelions down in one corner, which served as an elastic couch.

"This will do very well," said the old fairy to herself, as she rested on the dandelion sofa, after her labors. "I like it the better for being so dingy outside. The Blue Fairy can keep my tulip residence and welcome."

Next she trotted out to visit the Harvest Mouse in an adjoining field ; and she was careful that no one should see her movements when she made this mysterious visit. The Harvest Mouse had just crept into her nest, which was formed of neatly woven grasses, in the form of a ball, bound to several wheat-stalks.

Dame Mustard did not attempt to enter the nest ; she knew very well that the tiny mice were closely packed together inside now, so she contented herself with tapping on the stalk.

"Who calls?" said the Harvest Mouse, thrusting out her nose suspiciously : then she ran nimbly down to meet her friend.

"One cannot be too careful when raising a young family, there are so many enemies on every side," said the anxious mother mouse.

"Is your nursling safe?" inquired Dame Mustard.

The mouse nodded, winked her bright eyes, and

led the way to a low-spreading bush, under which
moss had been scraped together carefully ; and on
the moss rocked a cradle, made of a robin's egg,
containing the prettiest baby-fairy that ever was seen.

Now we may as well hear the whole truth of the
matter. Who do you suppose she was? Why,
Prince Parsley's own daughter, and Dame Mustard
had smuggled her away to the Harvest Mouse, during the war, and here she had remained ever since.

When the old fairy saw what a delightful retreat
it was, and how plump Elfie looked, she embraced
the good mouse so cordially that the latter was nearly
strangled to death.

"No thanks are needed," said the kind-hearted
animal, curling her whiskers. "I would have kept
her in the nest, only she is so different from the
mice that I feared the grass and straw would hurt
her tender frame, so I placed her on the soft moss
instead."

Had not the inhabitants of Shimmer been sound
asleep, they might have stared with amazement to
see Dame Mustard marching home to her tree-stump
mansion, carrying the sleeping Elfie in her arms,
followed by the Harvest Mice, father and mother,
walking on their hind-legs, solemnly, and bearing
the robin's-egg cradle between them.

They ate a few seed-grains and an earth-worm or
so, which the fairy prepared to suit their appetite,
while they rested, and then they ran nimbly home

again, fearing something had happened the young mice during their absence.

Dame Mustard did not intend telling any one who Elfie really was, for she was a scheming, plotting old fairy as ever lived, and she dared not have it known that her charge was of the royal house of Parsley, for fear King Doddle should order Elfie shut up in the acorn prison too.

At first Elfie was kept within-doors, but this could not last long as, she grew daily more wilful and mischievous : she was fast developing into a mad-cap fairy, occasioning her god-mother infinite trouble and anxiety. She was the most restless atom, never remaining in one place for a second ; fluttering hither and thither, and leading Dame Mustard such a dance to keep her from harm, that the sister Mother Pepper was sent for to come on a visit.

Mother Pepper was even older and more shrivelled in appearance than Dame Mustard, yet, if her nose was sharp, curving down to meet her chin, until she looked as much like Punch as it is possible for a fairy to look, her wisdom was very great. Elfie loved the two old ladies dearly ; still, she must have her frolics in spite of them. When she had gone to bed in her robbin's-egg cradle, Dame Mustard said:

" Well, what do you think of her ?"

Elfie pricked up her little ears, and opened one bright eye, for she was not asleep by a long way yet.

" She is not so bad," replied Mother Pepper reflectingly, putting on her beech-nut slippers. "Let the child run about more, it will do her good ; only make her promise never to visit the palace. She will keep her word, I know."

"Of course I will, you old dears !" cried Elfie, sitting up in the egg-shell. "Why should I not go to the palace, if I feel like it, though ?"

Dame Mustard was so startled that her cap fell off, but her sister had more presence of mind.

"We do not want you to go there, child," she said. "You belong to the Black Fairies, and if the king catches you he may use the acorn prison for a new inmate."

"Dreadful," whimpered Elfie, hiding her head under the violet coverlet of her bed, in affright. "I will never go there, I am sure."

The two old ladies nodded and winked at each other ; then they brewed a cup of something hot out of a bitter herb, that answered the place of *tea* to mortal old ladies, and went to bed, thinking they had terrified Elfie into keeping out of harm's reach.

The next day they went to make a call of ceremony on Dr. Mannikin, who lived in a mushroom at some distance away. He was esteemed the best physician in the kingdom of Shimmer, and had great knowledge in other matters as well. He had decided positively that the moon is made of green cheese ; at what period a new volcano may appear on the earth's surface; and the exact length of the last comet's tail to an inch.

Left alone, Elfie, wondering what to do next, thrust her head out of the door and found the air so sweet, the sun shining so delightfully, that she was tempted to do something amusing.

"I will not go to the palace, but I must have some fun elsewhere," she said, and proceeded to her god-mother's stable to select a suitable charger for an expedition out into the world.

There were two fat, sleek, well-conditioned beetles, four moths, with wings like velvet, a dragon-fly, and a handsome wasp.

"The beetles are slow," said Elfie; "the poky old moths would be sleepy in the daylight, I suppose; and the dragon-fly is a conceited thing."

"Take me, then," buzzed the wasp.

Elfie led him out of the stable, closing the door that the others might not escape.

"I don't need a bridle," said the wasp. "Get upon my back, and away we will go!"

When the two old fairies returned home Elfie was gone. Every nook and cranny was searched for the missing fairykin, but she was nowhere to be found, not even in the stable, where the fat beetles still stood.

"Has she taken that skittish wasp instead of any of you slow-coaches?" cried Dame Mustard in dismay. "She will never return safely; the wasp is such a rattle-pated fellow."

"Keep cool, sister," advised Mother Pepper, fanning herself with a blade of grass. " Elfie will come home when she is tired of rambling about ; and as for the wasp, his heart is in the right place."

Dame Mustard sighed, wrung her hands, imagining all manner of evil had befallen Elfie, while she had not come to grief at all, in reality.

The wasp spread his gauzy wings, the tiny maiden tucked her little petticoats about her, and away they sped out into the sunshine, the soft breeze rustling through the tree-tops, then dying away in perfumed breaths among the flowers.

"They tell me you are wild," said Elfie to the wasp. " If you do not mind me, I shall not take you out again for a month."

" I will be good," replied the wasp meekly, and he kept his word.

First they descended in a garden, where a fountain rippled over into a marble basin with a musical plash, and the shrubbery defined many a winding path. Elfie rested on a rose-bush drooping under the weight of fragrant clustering flowers, watching the spray of the fountain dash up in sparkling foam, while the wasp feasted on honey.

Some children came running along, and one little boy seized the blossom where the wasp clung in his chubby fingers, so that the insect should not escape. The wasp lost temper at once, and creeping out stung the urchin smartly, causing him to sob with pain. The other children endeavored to comfort him, but Elfie flew down from her perch, and kissed the poor little fingers, thus healing the cruel wound, although the children could not see her, for she had made herself invisible.

"Why did you sting the child?" inquired Elfie severely, when she had mounted the wasp's back once more.

"It was only in self-defence, little mistress," replied the irritable insect, whose temper had cooled somewhat by this time.

Next they alighted beside a brook that gurgled and trickled along merrily, now winding under the shadow of overhanging trees, then flashing out into the sunshine again. The wasp rested after the somewhat fatiguing journey, while Elfie fluttered about, and finally poised herself upon a floating lily-leaf far out on the rapid current.

A handsome trout, with metallic-tinted scales, thrust his nose out of the water to admire the delicate little maiden.

"You are very pretty," remarked the trout, rolling his goggle eyes admiringly. "If you will marry me we will have a delightful home in a hole under the bank, where the anglers shall not annoy us with their temptingly baited hooks."

"Thank you," laughed Elfie. "I do not like the cold water well enough to be your wife."

The trout inflated his purple gills and looked very salky over his rejection.

"In that case, come up here into the sunshine and marry me," chirped a locust in frosted green armor. "I can sing to you as well as most of my race."

"Do you call it singing to scrape your legs against your wings?" said the saucy Fairykin. "The tree-toad can trill better music than that."

"My son has a residence in the marshes near by, hung with rushes," said a large frog, swimming up to the leaf. "It would make you a splendid home, my dear. He is at present a melancholy widower, his bride having been caught to make some kind of a French pie.

But roguish Elfie only danced on the lily-leaf, and splashed water in the old frog's face; then she departed on the wasp-charger again, in search of fresh adventures.

An humble cottage nestled among low-spreading fruit-trees, with vines clustering quite up to the sloping weather-worn roof, surmounted by a clumsy toppling chimney.

The mother was busily engaged gathering purple plums into a basket, while the baby, a bright-eyed, round-cheeked mite of a thing, played on the grass.

Presently he toddled away, and the mother did not notice that he trotted straight toward the well, where the cover was half withdrawn. What if baby fell in? Elfie thought of that and quickly wove the grass blades together into a neat trap for his straying little feet, just before he reached the brink; so baby, not very expert in the art of walking yet, tripped up, fell on the back of his head with a bump, and gave a gurgling cry of surprise when he beheld the wide blue sky above him, which he had never noticed before—the world was so very new to him.

Mother shrieked with terror, and caught baby in her arms when she saw the danger.

"If you stop to set everything straight on the earth, we shall never get home," said the wasp, yawning wearily. "It is cold and dreary down here when night falls, I assure you."

The sun was already setting in a bed of purple cloud; still, Elfie was determined to see a large city before her return to the Shimmer kingdom. As they flew toward the distant spires and roofs the sun disappeared, the rosy clouds faded, and mist began to curl up over the river, like shrouded ghosts; evening had come, and the drowsy wasp flagged in his movements.

In the sultry city streets, where the gaslights flared like chains of glimmering stars, and the few trees of the square drooped parched and withered, the heat was most oppressive. Elfie crept into the open attic window of an old house in a poor street, where a sick child lay in pain and weariness upon a hard couch.

The child was patient and good; she lay there with wide-open eyes, thinking of the fresh smiling country, and longing for the sweet scent of flowers, while her grandmother nodded in the corner.

Elfie hovered above the little invalid, gently fanning her with her perfumed wings, until sleep weighed down the tired lids over the bright restless eyes, and a peaceful sense of rest relaxed the feverish frame.

In the mean while the wasp had gone fast asleep on the window-sill, and Elfie did not disturb his slumbers, but flew swiftly out into the country again, where she persuaded an owl to assist her, as the bird was so large.

Elfie stated the case to the whole owl family, just when they were starting forth in search of mice and moths for their supper, from their home in a hollow tree.   They all eagerly assisted in gathering flowers for the sick child, which were then twined about the mother owl's neck and under her wings.

"Nothing shall harm you," said the fairy, and soon they returned to the small chamber where the child still slept quietly.

Then Elfie laid the delicious roses and snowy lilies, with the cool green leaves, upon the child's breast, and their fragrance mingled with her dreams, so that she imagined herself to be in Heaven already

When naughty Elfie arrived home the next morning (the travellers having passed the night in a hollyhock), she found the two old fairies very anxious about her.

"I have seen something of the world," she said to them ; "and three offers of marriage were made me. What do you think of that ?"

Now came the grand Court ball, and King Doddle invited the Black Fairies to be present, as well as his loyal Blue subjects.

Mother Pepper and Dame Mustard were in a flutter about it : they decided Elfie should look prettier than any one else on that great occasion ; and Elfie herself, being a girl-fairy, was no less interested. If you could only have seen her when dressed in ball costume, the old ladies standing off to admire her through their spectacles !

Her hair was powdered with the gold dust from a butterfly's wing, collected at great expense ; her skirt was made from the sea-lettuce, bordered with a flounce of foam, and her boddice was formed of the green wing of a beetle, as brilliant as polished enamel. An opera-cloak of the same sea-foam was wrapped about her, and the three started in their close carriage, a walnut, in great style and splendor, for even a rebel fairy may keep a carriage, it seems.

Mother Pepper wore a gown of folded buttercups, suitable for her years, while Dame Mustard appeared in a chestnut-bur robe, so as to be as prickly and ugly as possible.

King Doddle's palace was one blaze of splendor; only, what do you suppose a fairy king's palace really consists of? Why, a ring of flowers enclosing a space of grass on which to dance in the moonlight. King Doddle and the queen occupied two full-blown red roses, the royal family each had a rosebud, and the courtiers, according to their rank, had violets, hyacinths, and pansy chambers, down to the lowly dandelion for the cook and scullions.

Elfie had never been so happy. The fairies danced and sang, then sipped dew and other refreshments. No one danced so gracefully or sang so sweetly as Elfie; at least her god-mother thought it, and the royal princes seemed to agree with her, for the five of them fell straightway in love with her, from the moment they obtained a glimpse of her slippers, embroidered with frost. The Crown Prince, especially, squeezed Elfie's hand, and whispered nonsense to her, which certainly was a kind attention, and the two match-making old Black Fairies looked wise at each other.

Next day the Crown Prince went hunting, and shot so many flies with his little bow and arrows, to distract his mind from thinking of Elfie, that the whole fly nation sent a remonstrance to the king. Then he took to slashing among the flowers with his sword, and did still more damage.

Finally, King Doddle drove in state to the tree-stump mansion to consult Dame Mustard. She told him that Elfie was of royal birth; and when he heard the good news, he concluded it would be sound policy to permit the Crown Prince to marry her, thus uniting the Black and Blue Fairies more completely under his sway.

On the wedding-day there was nothing but rejoicing and merriment throughout the kingdom of Shimmer; even the Harvest Mice appeared at the ceremony, wearing green cravats in honor of the occasion.

Dame Mustard was radiant with delight; and well she might be, for if she had not hidden Prince Parsley's daughter, how would the two rival factions ever have been united?

Annie's Valentine.

N a large city, sometimes called Gotham,
lived two little sisters: and this 's no fairy
tale, understand, but a "story founded on
fact," as the novels say. These two little sisters
were quite unlike. Lucy, the youngest, was very
pretty and sweet-tempered, because she was always
petted and caressed for her beauty. She was like
some sleek graceful kitten, with the fur stroked the
right way, and never rumpled the wrong. No wonder she was plump and good-natured! With Annie
the case was different. Her hair *would* not curl,
and so had to be clipped short, very much like that
of her brothers; her nose was a very insignificant
member; her shoes were always getting unfastened
somehow, or her apron awry, while Lucy generally
looked fresh and nice. If a stranger spoke to them,
Annie grew dreadfully shy, and hung her head as if

she was ashamed of herself; but Lucy answered promptly and clearly enough : so she became the general favorite.

Nobody besides mother really knew what good there was in the little plain one perhaps, although the boys declared she was a "brick," and made faces at prim Miss Lucy, who stepped about daintily and did not care to join in their games, while Annie could romp with the best of them.

It is very wrong to treat *one* child with more favor than the others in a family, and the good mother strove to make her love for Annie counterbalance the neglect and partiality of friends ; still, the poor little heart would be wounded sometimes, and she would wish that she was only pretty and clever, like the more fortunate Lucy.

The children went to dancing-school, and here the difference between them was more keenly felt than elsewhere, for all the pretty boys liked Lucy, who whirled about a lovely fairy under the dancing-master's approving eye ; and only the stupid clumsy ones ever asked Annie to dance, it seemed to her. She had *one* admirer, to be sure : what young lady of ten years has not? He was a tall thin boy, with pale yellow hair, and pink eyes, which made him resemble a rabbit, Annie thought ; and when he tried the polka he always got out of step, and then the master bade them do better quite severely, when Annie was doing very well all the time. She would

look wistfully at the elegant little men with curled
hair and gold watch-chains, Lucy's cavaliers, but
they seldom noticed her in return.

James Blake—that was the name of her rabbit
faced beau—brought a paper of candies to the dancing-school one day, and when all the scholars were
seated he came across the room to give them to
Annie. What do you suppose he did? Why,
slipped on the smoothly waxed floor, fell, and the
paper burst, scattering the sugar-plums in every
direction with a crash. How the boys and girls
tittered over the accident, while Annie's very ears
grew hot and red with shyness, knowing that they
were all looking at her! How angry the master
became, and ordered James to give him the package,
which he kept, too! Certainly Annie was a very
unfortunate little girl; still, she could go home and
tell mother all about it, and that was a great comfort.

We have almost forgotten to mention Aunt Katherine, who was spending the winter with the Holmes
family. She was an unmarried lady, very particular
about her tea's being strong in the morning, her
hair nicely arranged, and that the children never
came into her room to crumple her collars or ribbons with their meddlesome fingers. Aunt Katherine was a disagreeable old maid, the boys declared,
when she complained that the noise of their boots
made her head ache. Still, she had many good

traits of character, although she was so severe with
them. Miss Lucy found little favor in her eyes:
she found Annie more patient and thoughtful of
others, when the first shyness had worn away, while
the spoiled Lucy was sometimes sulky if she was
not praised.

"The nice boys all dance with me, and want
little bits of my hair to keep," said Lucy proudly,
tossing her golden curls. "You could not give
James Blake any, because you have none to snip
off, Annie."

Annie looked at her small brown head in the
nursery looking-glass rather doubtfully for a moment; but Robert, the eldest brother, who was doing
sums on his slate, looked up and said—

"It is a great deal more jolly not to be bothered
with curls."

Aunt Katherine sat before the fire with her work-
basket beside her, occasionally glancing at the children.

"If you are not good," she said to Lucy, "nobody will care much about your beauty, you will
find."

Lucy pouted and looked vexed. Aunt Katherine
did not seem to be a pleasant person at all. Before
they went to school the lady called Annie into her
room, and when the little girl came out again she
had a beautiful scarlet-velvet cross suspended about
her throat. All day selfish Lucy teased and coaxed

her generous-hearted sister to give her the ornament, until Annie yielded, and Lucy returned home wearing it about her own slender throat. Aunt Katherine's sharp eyes took in the whole matter, and she brought the little culprit to her amiable mother, who had been away in the morning

"You have many more gifts than Annie," said Aunt Katherine severely; "are you not ashamed of yourself to take this present from her?"

"She did not mind," faltered Lucy, pouting again.

"I gave it to her myself, please," put in Annie, anxious to save the other from blame.

"How is this?" inquired the mother, looking grave.

"Why, I gave Annie the velvet trinket this morning," said Aunt Katherine; "and before they returned from school Lucy had got it away from her. It is not right."

"Certainly not," replied Mrs. Holmes. "Lucy, give back the cross to your aunt, then there will be no more words about it."

This was too much for Lucy's wounded vanity. She tore off the ribbon and flung it at the lady, then burst into a flood of angry tears.

"You ugly cross old thing!" she sobbed, stamping her foot passionately. "Annie ga—ave it to me, but I do—n't want it."

I should be sorry to write all that naughty Lucy said on the impulse of the moment, how wickedly she screamed from pure rage, and even flung herself upon the floor because no notice was taken of her When it was all over, and the tempest had subsided, mother took her away to another room, after which she returned much subdued, to ask Aunt Katherine's pardon.

"As to that," said the lady, rubbing her sharp nose with one finger reflectively, "I can forgive you; only I would not advise you to give way to such a temper often, as it may lead you to do something very dreadful."

This all happened before St. Valentine's day arrived; for, next after Christmas, that was to be considered a great event in the Holmes family. The children talked about the matter together, as the time drew near, over their books at night when they were preparing their lessons for the next day. Willie could draw famously: he had received a prize for some sheep done in crayon the year before; and it was fortunate he won the medal in that branch, for he spent much more time drawing monkeys and mice upon the margin of his books than in studying their contents.

"I shall draw two horses in a farmyard for my valentine," he said, and began at once.

"What have horses to do with valentines?" laughed Robert.

"I don't care," said Willie sturdily; "somebody shall have them."

The weekly papers had wonderful pictures, which the children looked at with delight : Cupids cutting capers in flower-garlands ; pretty young ladies giggling behind window-curtains over poetry addressed to them ; servants peering up at the postman from the area steps, to receive their share in the day's fun · little boys delivering envelopes larger than themselves, then running round the corner ; and a world of nonsense.

"I expect to have lots," said Lucy, all good-humor again, dancing about at the prospect.

There was no holiday at school in honor of St. Valentine, so our little friends plodded along at desk and blackboard as usual, with charming pink envelopes and mottoes floating before their eyes in anticipation. At length they were released, and ran home eager to behold what treasures awaited them.

On the nursery mantelpiece lay three envelopes— one a delicate green, another blue, and the third a lace-work affair, with enough space in blank paper for the name of Miss Lucy Holmes. Some boy must have had empty pockets after that was bought ! They were all for pretty Lucy, not one bore Annie's name. Oh dear ! how hard it was to keep back the bitter tears ! how delightful it would have been if somebody had remembered her, also !

Hannah, the nurse, sat sewing by the window, where the canary-bird swung in his cage, trilling gay songs to the sun all day long and the ivy climbed over a frame from a Chinese flower-pot.

"The day is not half-gone yet," said Hannah cheerily, looking up from her work at Annie's troubled little countenance; "besides, *I* have not had a single valentine. What do you think of that?"

The children laughed.

"Your lover has gone to sea," said Lucy.

"Don't you really expect any?" inquired Annie eagerly.

"Of course I do," replied Hannah, whose face was still fresh and pretty enough to prove attractive, one would think; but she only said it to comfort Annie, and prevent her from crying, which she was very near doing indeed.

"I will give you this one, Annie," said Lucy, selecting one of the valentines, and intending to be very generous.

"No, I don't want to take yours," returned Annie; "it was not sent to *me*."

"If I could leave the baby," thought good-natured Hannah, when the children had gone to their dinner, "I would just run out and get Annie one myself."

The baby waked up while she was reflecting, his bright eyes sparkling, and his cheeks like two fresh roses; so Hannah could not leave the small master to himself, as he was old enough to crawl about after pins and needles, or fall into the fire.

At that very instant, had nurse only known it, Aunt Katherine and mother were in a large book-store, consulting with an accommodating clerk over valentines. When mother had decided upon one, the clerk very politely consented to direct it in a bold handwriting, with splendid curves and flourishes.

The children chatted together over their dinner about the important events of the day. Willie's picture of the horses had gone to some little sweetheart, who would easily guess where it had come from, by the spirited way in which the animals pranced their fore-feet. Willie's horses always did that. The boys were kind-hearted enough, but so intent were they on remembering the numerous little ladies of their acquaintance, that they had spent all their money before they once thought of the neglected Annie. James Blake would have favored her with two hearts thrust through by a gilded arrow on satin, perhaps, had he been there, but he had been sent away to a military school soon after the day when he spilled the candies under the dancing-master's eyes.

Dinner over, and the last remnant of rice-pudding devoured, the boys proposed they should go up into the nursery again, where baby was crowing and gurgling amiably at the world.

" Well, Hannah, have you any valentines yet?" inquired Robert with an assumed air of indifference, dancing on the hearth-rug to the baby's delight, who clutched at him with dimpled tiny hands.

"There is the door-bell now," said Hannah; "perhaps that is one."

The boys rushed out to seize the letter. Yes, it was for the nurse. Hannah opened it solemnly, amid shouts of laughter, as the picture of a very smart-looking young woman in a red dress and yellow apron, bidding a no less remarkable sailor in a blue jacket and tarpaulin hat, with a rose in his button-hole, good-bye, unfolded before them.

"There is the ship he is going to sail in," said Willie, looking over Hannah's shoulder while the others clustered round. "My eye! isn't he handsome though!"

"Where did it come from?" wondered Annie.

"Bless you, dear!" replied nurse, "these rogues did it. They were up to some mischief, I knew, when they came up stairs instead of running out to play."

The two boys laughed, and looked at each other in a guilty way. All this diverted Annie from her own sorrows for a time, yet the sad recollection returned again with even greater force afterward. Hannah's valentine afforded amusement to baby when the others had forgotten it; he stared with bab-yish gravity at the red and yellow clad young woman, and finally tore it to pieces suddenly. Again the door-bell rang sharply, and Annie's little

heart gave a sudden bound. Could this be for her?
No; it was a beautiful bouquet for Cousin Hetty
instead. The young lady bent her head over the
delicate flowers—waxen camelias, violets, fragrant
heliotropes, and roses blended together in gorgeous
array; but the children certainly thought that the
color flushed into her cheeks quite to her pretty
hair.

"Is that your valentine?" inquired Annie.

"I suppose so," she answered, then ran up stairs
with it.

The nursery clock struck four, and Annie began
to despair of St. Valentine's favoring her with any
notice whatever. The doll-house needed arranging,
and Hannah agreed to play for half an hour while
mother took care of the baby. It was always considered a rare treat to have Hannah play, partly
because she had so little time, and partly because
she was so extremely funny—in Annie's estimation.
Nurse did even better than usual on this occasion;
she took one of the kitchen dolls for a char-woman
to clean the parlor and dining-room. "She had
been hired expressly for this purpose," Hannah
said; "because the genteel waitress had broken
her china foot, and the cook had too much to do
already in making dishes of scraped apple and chalk
for the doll family."

There never was a char-woman who worked and
talked equal to this one. She turned out the little

piano, the tables, vases of paper flowers, and silk footstools, to sweep the velvet carpet; then she put them all back again, looped the curtains at the windows, and dusted the pictures upon the wall neatly

"What lazy things you all are up stairs!" she said. "If you only took off your gauze dresses and pink ribbons, the exercise of cleaning house would do you good; still, it is for my good after all, I get paid for the work, and I have five hungry children to feed in the next alley."

When the lady of the house came down to pay her, however, the char-woman was very respectful, received a slip of paper, which was supposed to be a bank-bill, quite gratefully, and departed. The parlor being so elegantly arranged, all the dolls came down stairs also to enjoy it, even to the small ones not more than an inch long. The daughter in blue, with crystal fringe on her flounces, was seated at the piano to make music while the others danced. How Hannah did make them dance, to be sure, singing a lively Irish air for the purpose! Up and down, round and round they went, guided by the nurse's fingers; even the aristocratic mother doll joining in, and tripping over some tiny baby dolls which ought to have remained in the nursery, where they had high tin chairs, with a bar to keep them in place.

Annie forgot everything except to laugh at Hannah's conversation, and the number of different

ways she made the dolls act. Next they went into
the pretty bedroom, with the toilet-table and glass,
the washstand, and ruffled linen on the bed. Here
stood a sewing-machine with a little brass wheel
which turned round, and the seamstress doll did
any amount of work, as Hannah made her stitch
long seams on the margin of bits of rag, ribbons,
cloaks, and sheets. Then they visited the kitchen,
where the cook was getting a famous dinner, the
table in the dining-room being spread with tiny cups
and saucers, knives, and forks, while a dessert waited
upon the sideboard—cherries, oranges, pies, and
ice-cream, all made out of painted wood it is true,
yet still presenting a fine appearance.

The dinner was never served, for just at that mo
ment the bell rang once more, and Willie came
into the nursery carrying a large letter in his hand.

"Is this Miss Annie Holmes?" he inquired with
mock gravity, as he made a low bow.

"Oh! Willie, is that for me?" exclaimed Annie,
dropping the frying-pans and kettles.

Yes, it was for her; Annie's valentine had come
at last. Aunt Katherine and Mrs. Holmes hastened
into the nursery, and Hannah carefully cut the en-
velope open, so that the little girl could draw forth
the contents, which she did with sparkling eyes. It
was three times as large as any that had been received
that day in the household; deliciously scented and
represented a wreath of roses with a bouquet of lilies

in the centre. Each little rose could be raised, like opening a tiny door, and underneath was a pretty picture framed by a line of poetry. The lilies in the centre concealed a mirror in a gilt frame, with a dove below, holding in his beak a scroll upon which was written, "To my Valentine."

Could anything have been more delightful?

"It must have cost ever so much," observed Willie.

Mother and Aunt Katherine looked at each other, but said nothing. Surely you would not have had them tell that they had seen it before, would you? Annie was wild with amazement and joy, she kissed everybody, even to the baby, and was seen to hug her favorite doll in the corner: altogether she behaved like a little madcap over her good fortune.

In the mean while Lucy stood gazing at the splendid valentine, a cloud of envy and disappointment settling upon her pretty features. It was so much handsomer than anything she had received—why should not she have had one just like it? Her mother noticed the frown, and whispered to her—

"Remember the velvet cross, and do not spoil your sister's pleasure again—she has waited all day for *her* valentine."

Robert was feeling quite blue because he had been reading a comic effusion addressed to himself, in which he was called a chimney-sweep. The rhyme was very good, yet it did not seem at all funny to Robbie, although he knew some other boy must have sent it out of pure malice. As he was a good-natured lad he put it in his pocket manfully, and came forward to admire Annie's present with the rest.

"What stunning writing!" he said, but they none of them could imagine where the valentine came from.

The firelight glimmered soft and warm in the parlor that evening, where the crimson curtains were drawn, and the gas sparkled upon a happy family circle, Annie still examining her treasure now and then. Why did Cousin Hetty wear such a rich silk dress, which shaded from gray to rose-red, like the changing light of an opal—poets would call it opalescent hues, but that is a very long word for little people ! Why was her hair curled and crimped in such a wonderful way? Why were her eyes so bright? Was Mr. Townsend coming to call, the gentleman with such beautiful black whiskers, and his hair parted in the middle like a girl's? Mr. Townsend *did* come, and Willie said—

"It is Valentine's day."

"Why, so it is," replied the gentleman; "I had forgotten almost."

"I guess you sent a smashing bouquet here to-day, though," said Young America, looking very wise.

"Willie, are you not ashamed?" said Cousin

Hetty, trying to frown, and she felt relieved when the children were all sent to bed.

So little Annie fell asleep to dream of the wonderful valentine, and she does not know to this day that the best friend she will ever have in this world —her mother—sent it after all.

THE TRAVELLERS' CLUB.

OLD Don, the mastiff, rose from the door-step where he had been taking a nap, shook himself, and strolled out into the barnyard to see if anything had happened to the ducks or chickens since he last made them a visit, for Don was the watchman on the farm.

The setting sun tinged the pine-trees on the hill-side above the house with a rosy light, and gleamed across the quiet valley, where the sleek cows were soberly wending their way homeward. The oxen were chewing the cud of rest, after a day of patient labor; the cock drowsily called his family to roost; and the birds in the trees softly twittered good-night to each other.

Don was not an admirer of nature; he was much more interested in watching his friend the bull-dog, as the latter dashed swiftly past the gate, holding a chicken-bone in his mouth, than the sunset clouds of the western sky.

"Bow-wow," barked Don. "What have you got there?"

"Never mind," replied the bull-dog, racing on toward his kennel, where he could enjoy the choice morsel.

Now Don was an excellent dog, as dogs go : still, he had some faults of his own, and he no sooner saw the chicken-bone than he longed to gnaw it himself. Accordingly he crept along to the next house, where the bull-dog belonged ; then, waiting a favorable chance, seized the bone, and galloped home with it.

Like any other thief, Don looked about for a safe spot in which to enjoy the stolen treasure, where the bull-dog would not search for him, and bounded into an outer kitchen built at the back of the house for summer use.

There was a large open fireplace, but the fire had gone out, and Don stretched himself comfortably upon the hearth never dreaming that he was disturbing a meeting of most important travellers.

A rat of great intelligence had squeezed into a small hole of the brick-work, at the appearance of this huge monster of a dog ; the bat had flown up chimney : and a tiny house-wren fluttered up on the window-sill for safety.

The rat felt that something must be done, so he thrust out his whiskers and said severely—

"You have disturbed a meeting of our club, sir."

"Club—dear me, what is that?" asked Don, winking lazily over the chicken-bone.

"Tell him to go away," called the bat down the chimney; then, as the mastiff did not move, the spiteful bat flung soot down upon the intruder's nose, which made him sneeze.

"Can we trust you?" inquired the little wren, hopping along. "A dog may have some manners, I hope."

"Well, then," explained the rat, emerging from the hole and stroking his gray coat smooth, for he was a wonderful dandy; "we meet here to tell our adventures at nightfall, and we call ourselves the Travellers' Club. The wren is president, the bat and myself are chairmen of the committee, and you may join if you like."

Don was so much interested that he quite forgot to finish the chicken-bone.

"Yes, we should be happy to have you a member," chirped the polite wren-president.

"We must be more select," snapped the bat. "Every animal should bring a letter of introduction, in my opinion."

The dog promised to be very quiet in his manners, and soon they had resumed their places; yet the bat disliked the visitor at first.

"What were you talking about when I came in?" inquired Don.

"We had not begun anything yet," said the rat.

"Perhaps you will favor us with some of your own experience, or adventures," said the courteous president.

The Dog's Story.

"I am the largest of the company, anyway," said the mastiff, crossing his paws comfortably, "and perhaps I should tell the best story on that account."

"Size does not make up for brains," said the bat, and it seemed to consider the remark a very wise one, if nobody else did.

"I am going to talk to-night, neighbor," replied Don, "as I have been invited to do so by the president here."

The bat said no more; and as for the rest of the Club, they were disposed to treat the mastiff with the greatest respect.

"I will tell you something about my own race, I think," continued Don. "We are a very respectable family—there's none better, and if there is one thing that I am proud of more than another, it is having been made a dog."

"You are first cousin to the wolf and fox, I believe," said the impertinent bat.

"What if I am?" growled the mastiff. "I have not said I was ashamed of my relations. Indeed I is supposed by some people that we originally *were* wolves, and when a dog grows wild he does become savage and wolfish.

"However that may be, we are spread pretty much over the whole world, which is more than you can say of your species, I dare say, Mr. Bat.

"The Greeks and Romans were fond of eating us. Virgil considered a fatted dog, served with whey or butter, quite a delicious morsel. We are used for food extensively still. The Chinese have dog-meat for sale in the markets; the Indians are not averse to it; and travellers in the Arctic regions, prompted by hunger, have made the same meal.

"I am glad that I live among civilized people, who treat me as Christians should.

"The Ancients also sacrificed dogs to their gods, especially to Mars, the god of war, and Rubigo, the goddess who presided over the corn. The dog Cerberus was supposed to watch at the feet of Pluto.

"In India there are many varieties of wild dogs, and among them the Dhole is the most celebrated.

"The dhole is built like a greyhound, and makes a famous hunter, often running down large fierce animals; although the dhole is sometimes killed in conflict with the tiger, elk, and wild-boar.

"The Pariah also inhabits the East. He has no home, and roams about, picking up a living as best he can.

"In Constantinople and Egypt troops of pariah

dogs take their own quarter of the town to them-selves, and if a stray one ventures on their territory they all unite to drive him away.

"The Greyhound is the aristocratic dog of us all, both because of his beauty, and for having been a general favorite from the Middle Ages, at which period the animal was frequently sculptured on tombs, at the feet of his master, as an emblem of fidelity.

"We are faithful : if men only treat us well, we will go through everything to serve them, while a cat is not to be trusted the length of my paw, for a good action.

"The Russian greyhound is called the Fan-tailed dog, his tail having a spiral twist like a fan.

"He hunts by sight as well as scent, the wolf and bear being easily overcome by a pack, which the nobility of Russia carefully preserve.

"The Persian greyhound is the handsomest animal of the two, having pendulous feathered ears, like those of the King Charles spaniel.

"He has great courage, and hunts in his native country the antelope, the wild ass, and the boar. The antelope has the advantage of greater speed, so the hawk is made an ally of the dog, and by flutter-ing in the deer's face, or darting sharp talons into his head, he is disconcerted, and the greyhound finally overtakes him.

"The Persians chiefly delight in chasing the ghookhan, or wild ass, a swift ferocious animal inhabiting the mountains which renders the sport exceedingly dangerous. The Persians place relays of greyhounds on the road, and show great skill, riding at full speed down precipitous hills, across ravines and streams in pursuit.

"The Dalmatian dog is a stylish fellow, with a spotted coat : you may see him in cities any time, trotting between the horses of fine carriages.

"The Cuban bloodhound was used by the cruel Spaniards against the revolted Indians in the West Indies. Cuba was said to have been made almost a desert, at one time, from the destruction of the natives by these dogs.

"Of course you have all heard of the St. Bernard dog—he has had such polite and wonderful things written about him. Living in the region of fearful snow-storms, where the convent upon the summit of the mountain shelters so many wayfarers, the dogs are sent out, with a little flask of spirits tied round the neck, to revive travellers.

"One of them, named Barry, wore a medal of honor : he had saved the lives of forty persons.

"There is a kinsman dog to be proud of !

"The Newfoundland combines the best disposition with fine strength ; he can perform greater feats in the water than any other dog.

"Among the many stories told of drowning people the Newfoundland has saved, is one of a vessel driven upon a beach on the coast of England. A heavy storm had raged and the surf rolled in furiously, so that no boats could be sent off to the poor sailors, who were signalling for help. Finally a gentleman brought his dog to the shore, put a short stick into his mouth, and directed his attention to the vessel. The dog at once understood what was expected of him, sprang into the sea, and struggled toward the ship, where the crew made a rope fast to another piece of wood, and threw it to him. The dog dropped his stick, seized the other, and returned to the shore with it, although repeatedly lost to sigh under the rough waves.

"A line of communication being thus formed, every man on board the wreck was saved."

"Splendid!" exclaimed the wren.

"I like all dogs except the terriers," said the rat, showing his white teeth.

"They are too sharp and quick for you even, I expect," said the mastiff.

"I once heard of a Scotch terrier that won a wager of killing twelve rats in twelve minutes. The second one fastened upon the terrier's lip and hung there while he killed the other ten."

"Come, now," interrupted the rat; "don't you call that a pretty good story?"

"You must not be prejudiced against a dog because he is your enemy," said Don. "But I had not finished what I was telling, quite. The Newfoundland is used on Chesapeake Bay in the capture of canvas-back ducks. At the dawn of day the ducks are to be seen securely feeding on the shallows, several hundred yards from shore.

"The dog is made to run after stones, which excites the curiosity of the ducks, so that they swim toward the shore to see what is going on. The dog takes no notice of the birds, until after the report of the sportsmen's guns, when he rushes into the water to arrest the flight of the wounded ducks, and brings them eventually to land.

"The Esquimaux dog is the most useful of us all, perhaps. When his master goes in pursuit of the seal, reindeer, or the arctic bear, the dogs carry the materials of the hunt, and the few necessaries to support life.

"Sometimes they assist in the chase, searching for the bear on land, and the seal along the coast. A few serve as beasts of burden in summer-time, carrying packs ; but the majority are set adrift to hunt for themselves.

"When winter sets in they return to their masters, and then their services become most important. I will not deny that they often behave badly, harnessed to the sledge, which they draw over the snow swiftly, carrying the family wherever they desire to go. One dog may worry his neighbor, and he, in turn, attacks a third, until there is a general state of confusion.

"The master must then adjust the traces and make the long powerful whip felt among the rebels; although even then the leader is his chief dependence, if the dog is obedient. The Esquimaux dog is famous for discovering the retreat of the white bear, when she suffers the snow to cover her, so as to form a snug vault, in which to sleep during the winter.

"The dogs having discovered the retreat of the bear, begin to tear up the snow eagerly, while the men dig a trench toward be animal, which is then struck in some mortal part with a spear, after which the young cubs that have never tasted blood, and are not therefore fierce, can be taken out without trouble.

"What prettier playthings for the parlor can be found than the Blenheim spaniel; the Maltese dog, not larger than a weasel; or the little white poodle of Cuba, which resembles a ball of floss-silk, with a pert nose thrust out from the midst of wavy hair?

"Poodles know a deal, I can tell you. They can be trained for almost any useful purpose.

"A poodle occupied a prominent place in the Peninsular War. He belonged to a French officer who was killed at Castella, where the French were compelled to retreat before they could bury their dead; but the poodle would not leave his master. Afterward a soldier tried to take away the cross of the Legion of Honor from the fallen officer, when the faithful dog flew at him so savagely that another soldier was forced to kill the animal with a bayonet before he would quit his hold. The poodle died game.

"Bow-wow! Did you hear a noise outside the window? Something must be going on that I don't know about," and out dashed the mastiff to see what the matter might be. He was the watchman.

They saw nothing more of him that night.

The chicken-bone, which Don had been gnawing before he began the story, lay upon the hearth unnoticed; still it had a word to say for itself.

"To talk only about one's own family seems to me poor taste," said the chicken-bone, loftily.

The others stared at the speaker quite astonished : to hear a chicken-bone express an opinion did seem surprising, certainly.

But this chicken-bone could do more than that ; it could tell a story with as much ease as any of them, and that was proved only the next evening.

Fortunately Mary had not noticed the bone lying on the hearth during the day, when the members of the Club were away, for they only appeared at night.

Perhaps Mary had been crying over the departure of her lover that morning, and so did not mind any disorder.

"If the dog will promise not to worry me, I can give you something entertaining," said the chicken-bone.

"Of course I promise," replied Den politely. "I can do that much, I should imagine."

So they all prepared to listen.

Experiences of a Chicken-Bone.

"I am a drumstick," said the chicken-bone; "I was once a part of as plump a fowl as ever graced a table. I do not know what has become of my mate, the other drumstick; we carried the chicken faithfully from the time it stepped into the world from the egg-shell, all its coat of yellow down in good order, to the day of its death.

"'Feep!' cried the chicken—we drumsticks were scarcely larger than lucifer matches at the time—and looked over the rim of the nest where the hen sat waiting for the other eggs to hatch.

"I suppose my time for running is over, although I have done plenty of it in my day, too. The chicken was never still a moment, when once it had crept out of that nest into the barnyard;—now scampering after stray grains of corn; now following the old hen into the tall grass which hid from view the brood; now racing for dear life to the coop, when barked at by the mischievous dog, until at last it was large enough to be fattened for market.

"Perhaps none of you ever attended a state dinner-party. I have, and I am going to tell you all about it.

"The chicken was killed and sent to market

Such a place for noise and confusion as that was ! There were fat-faced butchers in blue aprons, rushing about everywhere among the rows of dead turkeys, quails, and partridges, while fruit-venders jostled customers in their haste to fill baskets with fresh fruit, which they would then cry through the streets.

"It was quite shocking to see the poor pigs hung by their hind-legs to the high beams.

"The chicken next went into a kitchen, where it was plucked, singed, basted, and roasted to a fine brown. It was then placed on a dish with another fowl that was especially proud of it's own plumpness.

"'I never ate anything but bread and milk in my life,' said the stranger chicken, as we slid up stairs on a dumb waiter to the butler's pantry. 'That is the reason why my flesh is so delicate and fine.'

"A large number of people were seated at the dinner-table, the ladies elegantly dressed in silks and laces; and several children were present also, although they should have been in bed at that hour, to my thinking.

"The scene was beautiful. Upon the panelled walls hung rare pictures, some of deliciously tempting fruits, just like those on the table; some representing ducks paddling about in the water, or puffy yellow goslings with bright eyes. Through the partially open windows the soft air rustled the rich curtains, and waving tendrils of vines, which climbed from fancy baskets and Chinese vases to the gilded cornice.   Bronze cupids upheld the clock upon the mantelpiece, that chimed the hour in silvery strokes of tiny bells, while the mirrors reflected the frescoed ceiling.

"The people at the table had their talk together— the gentlemen about politics, the ladies on the last opera singers, and the children whispering together about when the ice-cream would come.

"We had our talk together, too, for that matter, and perhaps there was quite as much sense in our conversation as in theirs.

"It was a wonderful sight!   The gaslight shed sparkling rays over the basket of choice flowers in the centre of the table, dripped golden shadows among the dusky purple of the grapes, the velvet-pink peaches, and flashed upon the silver dishes.

"'I hope I am cooked enough to suit,' bubbled the turtle-soup, spitefully, in the great tureen.   'I only wish every one may have as bad a stomach-ache, after eating me, as the poor turtle must have had when they wrenched his shell-armor off.   Why could they not have left him unmolested in his native West Indies?'

"The soup talked until it had disappeared down every one's throat, and the tureen was removed.

"'We are never cooked,' said the Malaga grapes. 'It must be so unpleasant!'

"'You are squeezed to death sometimes, though, to make wine,' replied the tube-rose.

"'Dear, dear! will that happen?' whispered all the grapes together, in alarm, swinging in pendent clusters from the fruit-dishes.

"'Every one knows that we were raised as a hot-house for the table,' said a black Hamburg, wisely 'It is true that in other lands we are put to different uses. On the shores of the Mediterranean we ripen in perfection, as indeed do the juicy fig and fragrant lemon, warmed by the rich benignant sunlight.

"'How different these cold regions seem, where we only bloom under the artificial heat of a glass dome! We had a conservatory to ourselves—the vine on which we grew filled the whole place ; and such other plants as occupied the shelves below, feathery branching fuchsias, crimson-tipped waxen camelias, and lovely roses, were obliged to live in just the temperature which suited us best, whether they liked it or not.

"'If one must live cramped up in such a place, it is pleasant to be the most important plant. We are of great value in the world of commerce, I can tell you, whether prepared as raisins, or made into the sparkling champagne and rosy-tinted claret.

"'The Rhine is a large vineyard ; Spain would be comparatively poor without the grape ; while even in remote Transylvania we have been carefully cultivated for ages.

"'Talk about turtles!' and the cluster of black Hamburg toppled over the rim of the dish, bursting upon the table with the shock and its own importance.

"The waiter, in his white gloves and necktie, gathered up the grapes and removed them ; but one rolled toward a little boy, who was growing dreadfully tired of sitting still so long, and he popped it into his mouth when his papa was not looking.

"Next came the fish, a wreath of green parsley round its tail, which gave an elegant finish to its appearance.

"'I am very fresh,' said the fish. 'I was sailing about beneath the waters last evening, with never a thought of danger to trouble me, and now here I am, after being boiled almost to rags over the fire, served up on a large platter.'

"'How were all the crabs and lobsters down yonder when you left?' inquired the mustard-pot.

"'Teased out of their lives almost, poor dears,' said the fish. 'I met an old acquaintance in the kitchen just now, a lobster ; we were neighbors in the sea, and taken out for the same party, I should judge—only the lobster was placed on ice, instead of over the fire.

"'What is the sense of *that*, I would like to know, freezing the lobster and cooking me ?'

"The fish suddenly ceased speaking, for the silver knife had been at work, cutting it into slices, and now there was nothing left but the head.

"The turkey was wonderfully grand, partly because of his size, and partly because the dish was garnished with beautiful japonicas; which was very extravagant, and that the flowers thought themselves.

"'Ugh!' cried the japonicas, shrinking together as much as possible. 'Only think of being spattered with gravy!'

"At this the bouquet in the centre of the table nodded and whispered sympathy over the indignity, and even the vines by the window rustled angrily.

"'All to make a stupid turkey look handsome,' said the ivy, spitefully.

"'When he can be made nothing better than a stuffed bird after you are done,' added a creamy-yellow tea-rose.

"'How awkward he appears with his wings pinned back!' echoed a lovely heliotrope spray.

"These remarks were peppered upon the poor turkey before he could say one word in his own defence.

"'I am sure it is not my fault,' said the turkey, quite abashed by the sarcasms of the company. 'I care nothing about the flowers, only the waiter arranged them for ornament.'

"'To ornament such a giant as you are!' said a japonica, looking up at the turkey's crisp sides, and blushing a deeper red with rage.

"Whether it was done purposely or not, I really

6

cannot tell, but the turkey lurched over, and extinguished the impertinent flower.

"The wine-bottles must have their little joke, too, as they stood neck to neck on the sideboard, only the claret and sherry were in portly-looking decanters upon the table.

"Puff, bang! went a champagne cork, and the rose-tinted fluid foamed and sparkled into the slender-stemmed wine-glasses.

"'Ah ha!' gurgled the champagne merrily. 'I am only an imitation article.'

"'I wonder you are not ashamed to confess it,' gravely replied the claret, which came from France.

"'Not a bit of it,' laughed the champagne again. 'I shall be drank up before you are, now.'

"Sure enough, every drop was drained and considered delicious: so, as no one knew of the imposture, perhaps it did no harm.

"It makes me confused only to think of the number of things I saw that evening; the dishes rattled about, the waiters whisked hither and thither, and the voices of the gay company blended together.

"One old gentleman with a red face, like a full moon, and a bald head, ate so much that I should like to know if he ever reached home alive, as a matter of curiosity.

"The salads bobbed on, but they were minced so fine, with lettuce, chicken, cream, and I cannot tell how many other things, that they had nothing what ever to say for themselves; the scolloped oysters sighed mournfully because of the stiff coat of breadcrumbs they were compelled to wear; and the vegetables seemed hard of hearing.

"'We are the most wholesome and useful vegetable in the world,' bubbled the stewed tomatoes, complacently. 'We have been used in all ages.'

"'Are you more favorably received than we?' cried the sweet-corn. 'You have not half as much nutrition.'

"'For that matter, I come before either of you,' said the rice.

"All this while the salt remained silent in the silver cellars lined with gold.

"Finally it spoke, very slowly and distinctly—

"'I never heard such a wrangling and quarrelling as to which is greatest or best. It seems to me it would certainly be more refined and courteous if we did not all talk at once, saying such spiteful things.'

"'We have so little time, don't you see? I am going now,' interrupted a partridge, hastily, as it was carried away.

"'I am a foreigner among you,' pursued the salt. 'I came from Poland. The bag in which I made the voyage was really sent by mistake, in a cargo; but it makes little difference to me, one may as well be devoured in this part of the world as another, if one's destiny is to be eaten at all.

" ' I lived away down in the earth, where the day-light never penetrated into the vast caverns ; where no sound, not even the faintest vibration of the air disturbed a profound silence.   You would suppose I might have been allowed to remain there, since it was in the depths of nature's rocky heart ; but no, the enterprise of man discovered the hidden riches of a mine ; sunk shafts, drilled tunnels and pas-sages enough to turn their brains, I should suppose, and scraped out the salt for use in the upper world.

" ' I was not the common green salt, lying nearest the surface ; I belonged deeper down than the marl, pebbles, and sand—for I was the crystal salt itself.

" ' Working in the salt-mines is far more healthful than in the coal-regions, where such frightful explo-sions often occur, burying the poor workmen in ruins.

" ' In the deepest recesses, which are not well ventilated, hydrogen gas sometimes collects ; but elsewhere the atmosphere is both dry and pure.

" ' Only think of thousands of men passing almost their whole lives in such weary toil as digging away at the ragged masses of salt overhead, or standing in dark clefts to dislodge huge blocks !   How little people realize all the labor the commonest article of food costs to procure, as they eat it !'

" ' The silver mines produced me,' said the castor.

" ' I came from the iron mines,' chimed in the carving-knife.

" 'Not one of the people present think of it, although I am indispensable to health,' continued the salt ; 'bread, meat, and vegetables would be tasteless and flat without me.

" 'There was a splendid chamber in the mine, with a chandelier cut out of crystal salt, hanging from the ceiling, which is lighted on special occasions, such as a visit from royal personages ; and strains of brilliant music float through the place, whirling to distant ledges, then falling back from each crystallized point of the roof in a volume of sound.

" 'I belonged in one of the passages, decorated with shrines and saints, leading from this chamber to a subterranean lake, over the surface of which glistened a pale light as the waters rippled against the stone walls. Imagine the beautiful effect of showers of colored stars, forming arches of fire in the dark waves, and illuminating the rocks and precipices, when the miners use fireworks for the purpose ! I have seen nothing in the outer world at all to equal the imposing grandeur of my home,' said the salt, reflectively ; and the silver was of the very same opinion.

"The olives, plump and smooth, could not believe this.

" 'What should we be without the sun ?' they said. 'The fruits of the earth, ripened by the blessings of heat and light, are of some importance, too.   Stay down in such gloomy vaults as those just described, if you enjoy it ; we will bloom above you instead, and furnish oil from the ripeness of our abundance.'

"It was quite by mistake that I heard all this conversation," said the chicken-bone.   "My turn to be presented on the table came just after the turkey trimmed with japonicas ; but I was placed on a small table near the door, and forgotten by the waiters, so I heard the remarks of those that came after me.   When the dessert was being prepared, however, I was taken again into the butler's pantry, just in time to see the amber and crimson jellies, the delicious transparent candied fruits, piled in tempting pyramids, and the ices, frozen into diamonds, stars, and hearts of variegated colors.   They were all pretty frostwork things, but they did not look very sensible ; still, that could hardly be expected since they were composed only of frozen water, cream, and sugar.

"It is a wonder I ever came this far, after the dinner-party, where I, as a drumstick, remained untouched.   The cook gave me to a poor man, who started on a journey he was to make through the country on foot, and the food given by the cook served him many days.   One noon he seated himself by a hedge to rest, and in unrolling his bundle of provisions, I slid down the bank without his perceiving the loss.

"The bull-dog, nosing about, discovered so choice a morsel, and carried me to his kennel. After a time Don stole me, as he has already told you ; and that I do not regret, for I have enjoyed myself infinitely in your society."

They were all very much pleased with this story ; it gave them quite a glimpse of high society, as the wren justly observed, and even the impertinent bat declared himself delighted, while the rat's eyes twinkled like two black beads.

The following morning the house cat, soft and black as velvet, with a white spot under her chin like a ruffled shirt-front, came sidling up to the kitchen-fire.

The house cat had always treated our Club with the greatest contempt and indifference, and when she had been kindly invited to join them, by the rat, she spit at the chairman, instead of thanking him, as any well-bred cat would have done under the circumstances.

"I can find more amusement in hunting mice, or taking a nap curled up on the sofa," she had said.

Full of mischief, her wicked eyes caught a glimpse of the poor chicken-bone, and she dabbed her paw into the corner where Don had carefully pushed it with his nose, to draw it forth.

"Thief!" cried the rat.

"Thief yourself," replied Puss, nothing daunted ;

and then she went through all manner of manœuvres with the chicken-bone, just to aggravate the rat, pouncing upon it as if it were a mouse, shaking, then tossing it up in the air.

"If Don was only here he would punish you for taking one of our members, you bad cat," said the rat.

"Hard names break no bones," said the naughty kitten, whisking her tail. "Now I am off!" and she trotted through the door into the wood-shed, with the chicken-bone in her mouth.

Of course there was a great lamenting over the departed bone that night, and the good-natured Don tried to find the missing member; but this the cat took care he should not do, so they were left to talk over the many virtues and amiable disposition of the chicken-bone, just as people are always talked about when they are gone. The Club grew dull through much prosing.

On the third evening the bat felt disposed to be agreeable.

"The chicken-bone objected to much being said about one's own family; but as it has gone, I suppose I may follow the example of the dog here, and make a few remarks in defence of my species, although we are the most unpopular creatures in the world."

THE BAT'S STORY.

"Yes, it is unfortunate," said the bat, briskly; "nobody likes us at all. We have always been out of favor because we dwell in ruined walls or gloomy caverns, while in Eastern countries we often find our way into the sepulchres and catacombs of the ancients.

"Then, too, we flit about just at twilight, in our noiseless flight after our supper of insects; and that being the hour when the ignorant and superstitious imagine every white object to be a ghost, we have been naturally associated with hobgoblins.

"Men are growing wiser now, and are beginning to appreciate us somewhat, although ladies will scream if one of us flutter near them of a summer evening, fearing that we shall bite, or get entangled in their nicely-dressed hair.

"We do bite sometimes, that is a fact," said the bat, cheerfully, swinging by the hooks of his wings in the chimney corner, head downward.

"Dear me, don't you feel giddy?" inquired the wren anxiously.

"No," replied the bat. "This is the most comfortable position imaginable, if one is only used to it.

"Don was boasting the other night that his race was more widely spread over the earth than mine

I doubt it, for we are found almost everywhere. In England we have the funny title of Flitter-mice ; in France, Bald-mice ; and in Germany, Flying-mice.

"Homer wrote about us, and if you don't know who *he* was you had better learn.

"Bats used to hover about the Pagan temples, devouring the remains of the sacrifices. As the peacock was the bird sacred to Juno, the queen of Heaven, in Grecian mythology, so the bat was sacred to Proserpine, the empress of Hades.

"The wise men of modern times have found us curious and interesting in many respects ; so it is to be hoped prejudice will blind the world no longer, as far as we are concerned."

"Yes," interposed the rat, maliciously, "but you have some ugly tricks still."

"Allow me to finish, if you please," returned the bat in a very dignified tone ; "particularly as you—"

"I don't deny I am a villain," chuckled the rat, rapping the floor with his long tail. "Continue the romance."

"There is so much talk about daylight and sunshine ! I sleep through it all, hidden in an old tree, while some of my relatives even have a smaller, inner ear to close, it is supposed, so that their nap may not be disturbed ; for our sense of hearing is very acute, and of much more importance than our eyes, which are very small, like those of a mole, and deeply imbedded in the fur. When the last

sun's ray has vanished from the horizon and the
shadows begin to lengthen over the smooth lawns,
or creep in misty vapor along the river-bank, then
we flutter forth, refreshed and active, to make havoc
among the mosquitoes and other insects that would
occasion more annoyance than they now do, if we
had not such good appetites. No one thanks us
for the service we render in the destruction of insects in the larva state, which prey upon vegetation
in temperate climates even. Some of the hot countries where these insects swarm by myriads, could
not be inhabited but for us.

"On the margins of tropical forests the clouds of
mosquitoes are kept somewhat in check by us.

"Bats frequent towns and settlements where they
are useful, for not being fastidious or delicate as to
their food, they devour all animal substances, in
whatever condition, thus removing a great deal of
dangerous matter that might otherwise induce dis-
ease.

"In Java, the Roussette, or Fox-headed bats are
found, and they are among the very largest of our
species. The body of the roussette is the size of a
small dog, and is frequently used for food by the
Javanese, the meat tasting like rabbit, it is said.

"Well, the roussette can afford to be a dainty
epicure, living as he does amid all the luxuries of
the tropics: where every breath is laden with the
perfume of spices and flowers; where the forests are

tangled with interlacing ribbons of climbing plants, upon which bloom the orchids, like purple and yellow butterflies, and blossom with the magnificent scarlet cactus.

"The bats hang in groups during the day with heads down, and wings folded about them, upon the trees. When night comes they resort to the gardens and plantations, where they feast upon the most delicious fruits, melons, oranges, and cocoanuts.

"The natives are obliged, oftentimes, to protect their fruit by means of loose bamboo nets.

"The common roussette of the Isle of Bourbon and of France is only half the size of the former, and often flies by day, although much more active in the evening. It lives in the gloom of the forests, but at midnight comes forth silently to devour quantities of fruit in the gardens.

"In South America the Vampire bat abounds, and it has a very bad reputation, owing to a habit of sucking blood from animals while they are asleep.

"What would you have? we must live somehow, I suppose. Of course the strangest stories have been told about the vampires. They used to be represented as a kind of monsters that came stealthily forth when every one was sleeping soundly, and by fanning their selected victims with powerful scented wings, lulled them to deeper repose.

"Now this is as sensible as most fables," said the bat, indignantly.

"The vampire does attack the ears of horses and cattle, and the combs of fowls, causing a considerable loss of blood ; still, death is not occasioned by it. The inhabitants of Paraguay have no dread of these animals, although they frequently enter the houses and attack any part of the body left exposed ; but beyond a painful sensation, which may last several days, there are no ill effects from the bite. The Spectre bat is the largest of the vampires, and that is six inches long, with two feet of spread wings.

"The Leaf-nosed bats are peculiar to the Eastern continent and Australia. In England they are called Horse-shoe bats, the crest on the nose having a resemblance to the horse-shoe. They are not nearly so large or formidable as the roussettes and vampires. They live upon cock-chaffers, sometimes taking a sip out of other bats ; and the flavor of frogs is much to their taste.

"I belong to the most numerous class, with a name so long that I can scarcely remember it myself, and a bat should certainly know its own name —Vespertilionidæ."

"Good gracious !" exclaimed the wren.

"Your name is longer than your body," observed the dog, winking lazily.

"I suppose I must be something but a plain rat. I shall find my name in the dictionary before morning, depend upon it," and the rat cut a caper with his hind-feet at the very idea.

"We do not have long tails, or leaf-like appendages to the nose, like our distinguished cousins of southern climates, but are small innocent creatures enough, doing no harm that I am aware of. Every one cannot be great in this world—there must be large vampires and insignificant bats, just as there are powerful kings and plenty of little people with no rank at all.

"If I could have had my choice I would have been born great; but I was not consulted in the matter, so I first drew breath in a cavern near by, and clung to the body of my mother until I was strong enough to fly myself. We build no nests for our young.

"I go to sleep all snug and warm, in the winter; the snow and hail do not disturb me, nor the keen winds chill. Then, when summer smiles upon the earth once more, I sally forth with reawakened activity.

"We devour quantities of insects. A dozen beetles and a hundred flies make me no more than a substantial supper. We usually take our game on the wing—there is some skill in that! but we do not object to snapping up a few grubs and caterpillars, now and then, from off the ground.

"Some of us live in chimneys, where there is no fire; while we congregate in multitudes in the stone edifices of Europe.

"I have a distant kinsman in Kordofan that lives in the holes of the immense baobab-trees; and still another found in Mozambique, of a bright green color."

"A green bat must be gorgeous," growled the dog, confused by all the wonders he had heard.

"There is much in the world that we know nothing about," observed the wren, thoughtfully.

The Sunbeam's Story.

Suddenly a bright sunbeam flashed through the window, seeming to slant down a ladder of dazzling light into the darkened room.

The sunbeam was beautiful beyond description; his garments were gold, and his wings shaded from purple and blue to violet and scarlet, like the changing colors of a diamond.

"I am sent by my father, the sun, to pay you a visit," he said, "before we go to rest beyond the hill. The sun is the greatest traveller of all, therefore he should be received into your Club, only that he has no time for such things.

"Everywhere he is worshipped by mankind for bringing heat and light to cheer the cold world, which would always be shrouded in gloomy darkness but for his rich benignant radiance.

"We sunbeams are his children. When he

rises from his bed of gray vapor in the eastern sky, the fluttering of his rose-colored mantle announces the coming splendors of day, and the earth begins to awaken, roused by the shrill crowing of the cock and the music of the birds.

"We play about his chariot-wheels, or dance downward to kiss the dewy flowers just raising their heads in the meadows ; then ruffle the placid surface of the lakes, where the fog rises like a transparent veil, and melts away at our approach.   Yes, we sunbeams have many little duties to perform, while our father the sun shines upon all alike.   We seek out the sheltered depths of the forest, where the young birds peer eagerly over the rim of the nest longing to fly, and the pretty squirrels spring from branch to branch in merry sport ; or we penetrate the narrow dull city streets, and peep in upon pale, pinched children, who need us quite as much as the flowers.

" I remember a dingy shop in one of those streets, kept by an old woman ; she sold candy, gingerbread, and withered apples.   She had a little grandson, a cripple, and every day the old woman placed his chair by the show-window where we used to come at a certain hour, so that he could enjoy our visit ; and a frolicsome time we had of it, flickering about his curly head, warming his thin fingers, and flashing in his large thoughtful eyes.

"He used to talk to us, telling us about the glorious land he was soon going to, where he would not be a cripple any longer, and we readily understood him.

"'Up in the sky,' we sang—"'Up in the sky.'

"One day we found the shop closed; we could not even peep through the barred window;—our little playmate, the lame child, was dead!

"A great ship set sail from England, and on the deck the poor emigrants gathered for a last glance at their native land, until it faded into a mere line of cliffs on the distant horizon. The winds promised to use the ship gently, and bear her along on the trackless ocean with prosperous breezes, and we sparkled about the little children soon to be transplanted to the land of the West; but the moon grew ill-tempered, shrouding herself in heavy sullen clouds,—and every one knows that she rules the sea.

"The ship was tossed about rudely on the heavy rolling billows that upreared their crests on either side of the frail craft, as if about to crush her between their green walls; and the little children were kept below in the close sickening cabins, for fear they would be swept from the wet decks overboard.

"At length the ship reached her destined port in safety, and the children might step on dry land once more, to seek homes on the broad prairies, that offer such a tempting abundance to the gaze of the crowded countries of the Old World.

"I often visit them now as they play, ruddy and

strong, in the cornfields, yellow with ripening ears, or the waving acres of grain, dimpled by the shadows of passing clouds.

"Yesterday we entered a great church through the broad arched portal and stained-glass windows, shedding a glory of reflected light upon the dark aisles; the splendid pictures in massive frames; the statues of saints; and the choir-boys, swinging silver censers of fragrant incense. The priests flitted about in their white robes before the altar, the church-bells chimed sweetly, and the organ pealed forth a rich harmony of sound, like clear trumpet-notes, then died away in rippling echoes among the vaulted arches of the roof. It was all very magnificent.

"Sometimes I visit places of worship where there is none of this pomp and display, for the people are plain and simple.

"Last Sunday I was in a country church not very far from this spot. The air was soft and mild, so that all the windows were wide open, and I roamed about among the congregation; now resting upon the white hair of some hard-working farmer, who had occupied the same seat for fifty years, perhaps; now flickering over the gay flowers and bonnet ribbons of the pretty girls in the gallery.

"There was no splendor of decoration here; no floating incense, save the prayers of the good pastor and his flock. I noticed a little boy, seated between two aunts, quite old ladies wearing their best stiff silks ; and the little boy did not dare move for fear of crushing the fine dresses.

"The sermon seemed so dreadfully long! If he dozed, the aunt on the right-hand pinched his arm ; if he attempted to pop a lozenge into his mouth, the aunt on the left frowned, and tapped him with her large brown fan.

"A butterfly, with wings like soft brown velvet, strayed into the window, and circled about bewildered, affording amusement for a time : then the butterfly danced out into the sunshine again, and the little boy wished that the pastor would get through preaching sometime, that he could get a new book, containing pictures, in the sabbath-school library.

"We looked down upon the East with our warmest glance. Below us lay the ancient city of Damascus, where the shops displayed aromatic spices, perfumes, rare fabrics, glittering pipes, and porcelain wares : caparisoned mules and graceful Arab horses pranced along, richly attired men and veiled women thronged the streets.

"The Sultan's palace sparkled under our rays with a dazzling brilliancy of snowy marble, gilded dome, crested spire, and slender taper points against the clear sky.

"We also looked down upon a small hovel of the most wretched description, on the outskirts of the city, where dwelt a poor water-carrier, his wife, and son. The floor of the hut was paved only with earth, the walls were cracked and mouldering. The water-carrier was a faithful honest man ; but he could barely earn sufficient to buy a measure of rice and salt, labor as he would through the heat and dust of the day, bringing jars from a neighboring wood, where there was a well of fresh pure water.

"Sometimes the son, a handsome boy, was hungry and cried for more food, and the good man would sacrifice his own scanty portion to satisfy the child s wants, then creep away to bed, himself supperless, to dream of plenty.

" If every one of God's creatures was well fed, what a happy world this might be !

" 'When our son grows up he will have some good fortune,' the mother would say, proudly.

"At length the boy did become a man ; we watched his growth day by day, and he was employed to assist his father carry the water-jars to and from the city. Those more fortunate in the trade passed them constantly with stout mules laden, instead of themselves bearing the burden ; and young Achmet wished they also owned a mule—that would be indeed a step up on the ladder of fortune.

"One day Achmet arrived at the well about noon, and tempted by the delicious coolness of the spot, he reclined upon the grass, and soon fell asleep

While he slept, a curious little old man, with a long silvery beard, dressed like a pilgrim, appeared before him.

"The little old man told Achmet the most surprising fact. This wood held something more precious than the well of sweet waters, he said. for a noted robber, who had made himself the terror of the desert, where he plundered poor travellers of their merchandise and gold, buried his treasures on this spot.

"Achmet awoke and rubbed his eyes, wondering if all this could be true. We sunbeams did not know, for the robber must have buried his wealth at night, and only the moon would be able to tell what happened, in that case.

"Achmet counted six trees, turned to the right, and discovered a rock, as directed in his dream, from which he scraped away the moss, and beheld a smooth block inserted in the earth. This he raised and found an iron chest beneath, containing sparkling diamonds, lustrous pearls, emeralds of liquid transparency, sapphires, and rubies. Nor was this all : solid bars of gold and silver, inlaid amulets, signet-rings, and glittering coins lay below. Achmet's eyes were dazzled by the glinting glowing mass of riches, that sent forth myriads of starry rays into the day.

"The water-carrier and his wife were quite bewildered by their good fortune, and it was not long before the son removed them to a home of splendor and luxury.

" They now live in a palace equal in grandeur to that of the Sultan. We often dance through the arched halls, the pavilions gorgeous in coloring and ornament ; down balustrades wrought in delicate designs to a semblance of lace, into terraces blooming with jasmine-vines and lotus-flowers, exhaling fragrance from their alabaster cups.

" I must tell the whole truth : we are cruel in our scorching heat in the desert, that spreads waves of yellow burning sand on every side, as far as the eye can reach. You can have no idea of such places here, where we are blessings to the fruitful blooming earth.

" A caravan of merchants started from Bagdad in brave array. The camels were laden with packages, the richer merchants rode fleet horses, and the line of animals soon wended their way out of the city gates. In the company were stately Turks, accompanied by numerous slaves, dark-featured Arabs, shrewd long-nosed Jews, and even Greeks, all absorbed in their own affairs and personal interests, yet ready to defend each other from any common danger which might threaten the whole company.

" The way grew toilsome and weary, as the patient camels plodded on, step by step, through the loose the desert burned under our fierce light, without shade of a green tree; and the heated layers of air radiated in tremulous vista of mirage, extending like refreshing lakes before the thirsty travellers, only to torture them by the receding delusion.

"All might have gone well with them had not the south wind begun to play his pranks, with sharp puffs of hot air, like the blast of a furnace, that whirled the fine sand in eddying columns, spinning rapidly toward the caravan. The camels stood still, terrified at the approaching storm, and the merchants drew their caftans close over their heads; still, the whirlwind overpowered them, horse and rider alike, and they were buried from sight under a monument of sand.

"Such sad events often occur : it is not our fault, however, for the south wind does all the mischief.

"We sunbeams are not afraid of cold regions. We glide over the dazzling snow-fields, the massive blocks of ice piled into glaciers, and the green valleys at the base of the mountains in Switzerland.

"The chamois-hunters are sure-footed enough ; they learn to climb and cling among the smooth rocks, and beside sloping precipices, where some river bounds along below, loosened from the ice-fetters which have bound it for months—a foaming torrent. But sometimes travellers slip into concealed clefts, powdered by a light fall of snow, down, down where the frozen walls of ice gleam pale-blue and green, like pure crystal. The sun never penetrates to those gloomy yet beautiful regions—it is always winter there.

"We love to tinge the rugged pine-trees with a purple bloom, and linger upon the tranquil lakes, while the clouds above, and snow-peaked Alps piled up in the distance, blush crimson under our good-night caress.

"Two little brothers lived in Chamouni, at the base of Mont Blanc. Their father was a guide, and he had gone up the mountain in a party with some adventurous Englishmen, who employed many men to carry provisions for the severe cold they would find up there in the keen air.

"All day the two little brothers, like many other children, had carried trays of carved trinkets, wrought by grandfather at home with patient skill—tiny peasant-women in broad hats, funny little bears of dark wood, with knapsacks strapped on their shoulders, and miniature Swiss cottages, complete even to the cow-shed and balcony—to sell among the strangers. They had made a great deal of money, and when father returned home down the mountain they would tell him all about it.

"Eagerly the children ate their supper and hastened out to watch for the appearance of the party. Other groups were waiting too—mothers whose sons were among the guides, and anxious wives. There was also an elegant foreign lady from the hotel, watching with the rest. Somebody said she was a sister of one of the gentlemen ; and the children looked admiringly at her rich dress, so unlike their mother's woollen costume, and her slender white hands, glittering with valuable jewels.

" The two brothers thought how splendid it would be to hear the cannon boom and see the flags wave, when once father was in their midst safe : they did not notice the anxious looks of the crowd, as the evening shadows closed about them.

" We heard the sad story next day. Out of the gloom of the evening came only three men, and there were no flags waved in their honor ; they were met only with sobs and tears. There had been an accident on Mont Blanc, a rope had broken which bound the party firmly together, and the foremost of them had slid with fearful speed to the brink of a chasm and vanished.

" The two little brothers went home, weeping bitterly ;—father would never come down the mountain, now, to hear about the success of their sales that day, and have the cannons fired for him.

" The snow-mountains seem even more cruel than the desert."

The sunbeam had been gradually fading, as his story drew to a close—it seemed as though the sun was warning him not to be delayed long, after the rim of his chariot had disappeared beyond the horizon.

" I could tell you much more of what I have

seen, friends," he said, cheerfully, "only I shall be late, if I remain much longer. Perhaps I will look in on you again sometime, and in the mean while I will wish the Travellers' Club prosperity."

So saying, the beautiful sunbeam floated out through the window again and sped toward the west, like a golden arrow of light, and disappeared in the radiant train of its father, the sun.

The Club felt very much flattered by the visit from so distinguished a stranger.

"A great compliment to our little circle, certainly," remarked the wren-president, ruffling his soft feathers.

"His appearance was dazzling," added the sober bat.

"He told wonderful things," echoed the rat, thoughtfully.

They were quite agreed that they had gained many new ideas of the outside world from the sunbeam's conversation.

As it was still early, the rat was invited to make some remarks.

"There has been a great deal said about family, by the dog and bat, so I may as well mention my own, I suppose," observed the rat. Then he commenced.

THE RAT'S FAMILY.

"We are an ancient and respectable race, said the rat, with a sly glance at the mastiff. He was a roguish fellow.

"Almost as old and respectable as those of my friends here—and there is everything in family, depend upon it! I have consulted the dictionary at the risk of my neck, for all the cats and dogs were after me before I accomplished my purpose. My grandfather lives in the barn of a wise gentleman, not far from here, and in his library I should find the other name, besides my plain rat-title, I was informed.

"I gnawed my way through the dictionary to the letter R, and when I found the class under which I was ranked, I carefully swallowed the word, so that I might fix it in my mind; but it has sadly disagreed with me, and produced an attack of indigestion."

"I never before heard of a rat's suffering from dyspepsia," exclaimed the bat. "But is your name as long as mine?"

"Well, no," returned the other. "Still, it has rather a more stylish sound—I belong to the order Rodentia, although it has given me a heartburn for eating it up.

"I find in the dictionary that we rats entered

Europe during the Middle Ages ; the brown species belonging to Persia, where it lives in burrows, swam across the Volga at Astracan, after an earthquake.

"We roam about under ground in the great cities, in the sewers, and through the mud of the docks, where we are very fierce, often attacking men ; yet you never see a rat, even in these places, without his coat brushed into perfect order, as though he had just stepped out of a bandbox, to use a popular saying."

"What vanity !" exclaimed the bat, again.

"Our soft fine skins are made into kid gloves for ladies' dainty hands, at all events," continued the rat, "which is more than your small body will ever amount to. I consider that a rat dies covered with glory, partly because he holds his ground well against enemies, and because his skin afterward appears to advantage in fashionable circles as a glove.

"The Musquash is a relative of mine : he is a water-rat. When winter comes and the river freezes over, he builds a little hut of earth on the ice, leaving a hole to dive down to the bottom for a favorite root, on which to feed."

"When the river freezes still more firmly and the roots can no longer be reached, the rats devour one another," said Don, quietly. "You did not tell that."

"Eh ! Did you speak to me ?" piped the wren.

sleepily; it was late for the little bird to be out of the snug nest.

"Only give me time, neighbor," said the rat "To be sure, the strong musquash may devour the weaker; but then the large fish eat up the little fish, the large animals the smaller ones, and the birds of prey are all alike.

"The Beaver is also a connection of great reputation; one hears about nothing but the sagacity and wisdom of the animal in building dams, chopping down trees, separating them into lengths, and treasuring the tender bark in their storehouses for future use.

"Certainly the beaver cannot be praised too highly. for his industry, if nothing else; and his habits of neatness are no less commendable, since he allows not even a stray twig to disorder his lodge, but carries everything of the sort outside the entrance to float away on the stream.

"Formerly the beaver was hunted for the fur very extensively, not only by regularly established companies and the expert Indians, but by independent bands of trappers, who passed their lives in the wilderness of the Rocky Mountains.

"The Prairie-dog lives in the far West, where the vast herds of buffalo sweep across the plains in flight, with flashing eyes and waving manes, until goaded into defending themselves or making an attack, by the arrows of the Indians showered into their midst.

" Perched on curious mounds outside their dwellings, the prairie-dogs sit barking at the world, and peering at any strange object, with their bright eyes, then if danger threatens they pop down into the earth out of reach.

"The little animals cannot always escape from danger in that way, however, for a rude owl insists upon living in the prairie-dog's dwelling, where the young owlets are treated to one of the tender marmots now and then.

"Besides bearing this intrusion patiently, an ugly rattlesnake must be entertained as well ; and of the snake the poor dog must be still more afraid, as a dangerous enemy.

"The Porcupine of Sicily and Spain, all bristling with black and white quills, is a cousin of mine.

"The mice belong to our race, although they are such small insignificant creatures that we do not think much of them. Have you ever noticed a beautiful gray fur, worn by ladies in winter?—not the common gray-squirrel coat, but a soft fine down. That belongs to the little Chinchilla, a native of the Peruvian Andes."

The rat paused, his whiskers twitching with suppressed anger : he had discovered that the wren-president was fast asleep, a mere rumpled little ball of feathers, instead of listening to his remarks.

"Go on," urged Don.

"I have nothing more to say when my audience

go to sleep, thank you," said the rat, giving an in
dignant sniff. "I think I will go down cellar, where
I have a bit of tallow stowed away for supper.

"Don't get vexed so easily," said the dog. "The
wren should be in his nest at this hour, while you
and the bat feel the brightest at night."

"I am not asleep at all," snapped the wren, wak-
ing up and feeling very cross indeed.

The rat felt seriously offended, the wren rather
pettish from keeping late hours, and it might have
taken more than the dog's good-nature to mend
matters had not another visitor appeared upon the
scene, at the moment.

The moon had thrust her rim up in the clear
heavens almost before the last sunset cloud faded
from the western sky, and now one of the pale beams
glistened through the opposite window, just as the
sunbeam had done.

The moonbeam was not less beautiful than the
sun's messenger. No bright colors flashed and
shimmered from his gauzy wings, only a pure silvery
lustre gleamed about him, transparently delicate as
hoarfrost, and a star of light shone upon his fore-
head.

The Moonbeam's Visit.

"The moon has risen over the sea, marking her
course with a broad tract of rippling silver on the

murmuring waters, and while she pursues her glorious way, I have been sent to pay you a visit," said the moonbeam.

"No doubt the sunbeam has dazzled your imagination with a vivid description of the day: he tells of nothing else. I can lead you to think of far different scenes, however : then you must judge for yourselves which is the most beautiful—night or day.

"Think of the delicious coolness and quiet of a moonlit evening, when the refreshing dew clusters over the parched grass, the breeze sways the high tree-tops, and a thousand sweet odors rise from meadow and garden, after a sultry day of intense heat : the sun's yellow glaring light penetrates through closed window, and the deepest forest shade, with resistless power.

"The moon sailed above the broad bosom of the Mediterranean ; now resting on some little village rising steep, roof above roof, on the hillside, or the fisherman's craft drawn up to the shore ; now darting mellow rays through the orange and lemon groves, powdered with snowy blossoms ; then reflecting her fair face in the bay of Naples, where the azure waves kiss the strand.

"We did not linger long on the fortified height of Gibraltar, or the distant shore of Africa, where the fierce Barbary pirates used to lurk ; we must pass on to the seat of former glory and lingering magnificence—in ruins—Rome.

"Through the deserted arches of the Coliseum— where the heathen throng used to flock, tier after tier of eager faces, to witness the gladiators' brutal combat, and the Christian martyrs thrown to wild animals, the crouching stealthy tiger and savage lion—the moonlight fell; over the once stately palace of the Cæsars; the Appian Way, where the tombs wend away into the distant vast sweep of the Campagna.

"It was a season of festivity, the streets were filled with a gay crowd, all watching eagerly for the splendid illumination of St. Peter's.

"The poor men, whose perilous task it was to light the lamps, suspended at intervals over the large church, had all received pardon for any sin committed during their lives, before they went to work, in case any of them should fall from the giddy height, according to the belief of the Roman Catholic Church.

"Suddenly a ring of flame twined about the dome, each little jet of light flashing into existence at a given signal, and the whole immense edifice was drawn against the sky, like some radiant palace of fairyland. It was a dazzling sight to mortal eyes, no doubt, and a murmur of delight rose from the enthusiastic crowd on the still air; but to the moon, far above, it looked insignificant enough, like a mere outspread flower, studded with flashing jewels.

"There is only one thing man has achieved that

8

is worth mentioning, in my estimation, and that is photographing the moon by her own light, after the telescope has discovered myriads of starry constellations, which are almost invisible to the naked eye."

The dog could not but consider this rather a vain speech, when man is constantly developing those gifts of the intellect which God has given him ; still, Don was wise enough not to interrupt the moonbeam.

"Sometimes the moon glides up the Nile ; she knew the source of the sacred river of the ancient Egyptians long before Captain Speke succeeded in penetrating to its cradle.

Acacias and tamarind-trees bloom there, the crescent of the Turk glitters on the temple spires and mosques of Alexandria, where the natives sit outside the houses during the evening, sipping their coffee and enjoying their pipes.

"Further up the river the date-palm lifts its feathery crest, a broken pillar rises here and there on the bank, to mark the site of some former palace, and the pyramids tower against the far desert, where the ostrich rushes along swiftly as the wind, and the marble sphinx has toppled over in the sand.

"A great people once ruled here, learned in every art and science ; but they have passed away, while the moon still pursues her course.

"In the sunny South the moon loves to linger, everything is so fragrant and beautiful. The Alhambra in Granada is one of her favorite resort , she may visit every nook in the gorgeously colored halls without meeting a living form, where everything used to be joyful with life ; for the dark-featured Moors, with their prancing war-horses and silken banners, their costly robes and jewel-hilted weapons, are gone ; so the moon must pass over the gilded cupolas to seek the sheltered balcony, where the musical tinkle of the guitar is heard, the delightful orange-groves, and the groups of young people dancing under the trees, their merry laughter rising sweetly on the air, to find the living and happy ones.

"In the large cities the moon is not appreciated as she should be. Few look up at her when she shines between the ranges of lofty houses—they are content with the earth alone ; she only serves to economize gas in the street-lamps.

"The little beggar-children, who have not sold all of their small stock of matches and pins, are afraid to return home, so they crouch upon some cold doorstep, hungry and weary, and lift their little faces to gaze at the moon, sometimes vaguely wondering if that is really another world, and what makes it so bright, until they fall asleep to dream of comfortable homes.

"The wealthy people are gathered at splendid balls, where rich colors blend together, as gay forms move about, and the music breathes through the large apartments. The price of the exquisite flowers, drooping and fading in the heated atmosphere, would make so many of those little beggar-children happy ! But the elegant ladies do not seem to think of this, or that God will surely call them to account for not doing their duty on earth.

" If the moon deigns to smile upon the sport, what a brilliant sight the ice presents, when the skaters steer about over the smooth surface in circling flight, like birds ! Ladies skim along gracefully, or recline in pretty ice-cars, nestled amid the soft warm furs ; and the children fly past, their fair hair streaming on the wind, while strains of martial music seem to keep time with the flashing of steel-clad feet, the ripple of laughter, and the merry jingle of sleigh-bells.

"What would the long dreary Arctic night be without the moon, when the ships that have penetrated to those desolate regions are firmly locked between fields of ice, and the poor Esquimaux burrow in their wretched hovels from the intense cold ? The sun no longer tinges the rugged mountains or the iceberg's glittering surface, tinging it emerald-green, pink, and purple, until it resembles some radiant sunset-cloud : the brief summer is past, and the moon shines with a peculiar steely clearness, seen nowhere else, changing frostwork and pinnacle of ice into a semblance of crystal castle and cliff. The polar bear, in a shaggy coat of white fur, prowls along the shore in search of prey, or suffers the snow to cover it, thus forming a snug warm cell in which to sleep through the winter; the ermine owl, no less warmly clad in soft feathers, soars over the waste to favorite haunts in the mountains of Greenland; and the agile cunning little foxes avoid the traps set for them.

"The Northern Lights form arches of rosy flame across the sky, resembling splendid vivid rainbows, from which shoot stars and rings, like fireworks, then fade away to a green line on the horizon again.

"Over the broad steppes beyond Siberia, where the Kirghis tribes pitch their tents, surrounded by their flocks like the patriarchs of old; where the Amoor rolls its dark waters to the countries of the East, the moon came to look down upon the city of Moscow, crumbling into flames before the advancing army of Napoleon.

"The ruddy glare of the conflagration lit up the sky, and even paled the moon's splendor for a time, the seething crackling waves of fire breaking against swaying tottering walls; then twining up the tower of the Kremlin, where hung the great bell.

"That was well done; the conqueror should find nothing but blackened ruins and ashes, when he entered the city at last.

"I must follow the moon to the western lakes and the great Mississippi, now; so good-bye for the present, friends," concluded the moonbeam, and resumed its journey out into the night.

The bat and rat were of the opinion that the moonbeam was quite right in considering night better than day; but the wren still thought the sunshine desirable.

The rat produced four nut-shell drinking-cups, filled with the farmer's best cider, from a cask in the cellar, and these he presented to the company.

'Let us drink to the health and success of the Travellers' Club," he proposed, and they all sipped the delicious beverage, except the dog, whose nose was too large to enter the tiny shell, and he tipped it over with his clumsy paws, instead.

"We need not go home yet," piped the wren, hopping on one leg, for the cider had got into his head.

"Certainly not," cried the bat, jumping down upon the hearth to show how the polka should be properly danced.

Don would have liked to dance, too, but he could not, for fear of crushing his small companions; and besides, his cider was spilled.

The wren went home to his nest, and was scolded by his little wife for staying out so late.

"You should set your family a better example, if you have no regard for my feelings," she said.

Old Don roamed out to see if there was anything worth barking at, to be found.

The rat frisked off to the cellar to enjoy the br

of tallow, and the bat spread his wings in pursuit of mosquitoes.

So we take leave of the Travellers' Club, hoping that they may derive much pleasure and profit from each other's society.

The Adventures of Tiny.

 Maltese cat, of very good family, was brought to town because of her beauty and elegance.

Although she was treated with every attention afterward by the whole household, the city air did not agree with her at all, so she went into consumption, and died genteelly, as became a Maltese cat.

She left one kitten, named Tiny, and it is about him we are to hear.

Tiny had a silvery-gray coat, soft as down, dainty paws tipped with white, and a spot under his chin like a ruffled shirt, which gave him a very stylish appearance. He was quite delicate, like his mother; if he did not have his meals served at a certain hour, he lost his appetite; if the beefsteak was tough, it gave him a fit of indigestion; and if he was served with cold milk, instead of weak tea in the morning, it made his head ache for the day.

All these trifling peculiarities are a sign of high birth in a cat, I assure you.

Once Tiny ran out on the doorstep when the servant was sweeping, and a little beggar-boy shouted, which made the kitten faint away on the door-mat, so that the young lady mistress was obliged to hold his head under the fountain-spray before he revived.

Certainly the Maltese lived in clover, for instead of roaming about in search of a living, as so many cats do, he reclined upon a silk cushion in the parlor, with a red ribbon cravat about his neck, and received calls.

One warm day in summer the kitten ran out into the yard to see something of the world, and, discovering a hole in the fence, crept through the space into the next yard, which was sufficiently large to be termed a garden, as there were several fruit-trees, an arbor covered with vines, and beautiful flowers planted in the border.

"You are pretty," said Tiny, blinking at a gorgeous crimson rhododendron, standing stiff on the stalk.

"We are more delicate and rare," rustled the roses, angry that any notice should be taken of a common flower.

Tiny dabbed a roguish paw among them, and

shook down a cloud of perfumed petals, then whisked on.

Suddenly the inexperienced kitten saw a splendid bird approaching, with green, yellow, and burnished purple feathers shading together in the sunlight.

"I am the cock," it said proudly.   "How I do love to crow when the dawn tinges the east! It is not like being answered by other cocks for miles around, in the country ; still, it serves to wake up people, and make them cross.   A young gentleman in the third story yonder throws boots, sticks, and even glass tumblers at me ; but I dodge them all, and only crow the louder, so it really does no good."

"I have never been out of doors before," said Tiny, cutting a caper.   "Does the sun always shine ?"

"No," replied the rooster ; "sometimes it rains."

"I don't know what that means," said the kitten.

"You would know if you felt it. One has to stand dismally under shelter, with one's feathers all ruffled.   Let me show you our house," and the cock very politely led the way to the stable, in the rear of which the fowls had an inclined plane to walk up into their home.

"Here we roost on comfortable perches," he explained ; "and there the hens lay eggs in boxes, so that the old gentleman can have a fresh one for his breakfast."

"You never catch mice, I suppose," observed

Tiny, not in the least interested in the hen family, and their mode of existence. "The kitchen cat tells me that is the only sport worth living for."

"That is viewing life from a cat's standpoint," said the cock, flapping his wings. "We have horses in the stalls with skins like satin, and such long tails! But perhaps we had better say a word to the parrot."

The parrot's tin cage swung from the balcony, and there sat the bird, gayly dressed in green, pecking at a lump of sugar.

"Good-morning," said chanticleer, hopping on one leg. "How is your throat?"

"No better," croaked Polly, cocking his head aside. "This climate has ruined my voice."

"He never had a fine one," whispered the rooster to Tiny.

"What are you saying?" cried the parrot. "I do not make such a noise as you do, if there is any beauty in that."

The cock was good-natured, but he could not keep his temper now, when *his* voice was mentioned in slighting terms.

"Cock-a-doodle-do-o!" he shrieked, turning very red in the comb with the effort he made. "What do you think of that?"

Poor Tiny was so startled by the noise that he scampered up the grape-vine, where he sat trembling with terror.

"You have frightened the visitor," cackled the parrot.

"I see a white bird in a cage on the ground," said Tiny, looking over the fence beyond. "Are you a parrot, too?"

"No, I am a goose," replied the bird, in melancholy tones. "Here I sit quacking over my sorrows, waiting to be killed and cooked by the Jew family, while my brothers are swimming about in the pond enjoying life."

"How very sad!" observed Tiny, and had time to express no more sympathy, for a stout servant, having a hooked nose, came out with a carving-knife to kill the goose, and Tiny sprang back into the rooster's dominion again, fearing his little head might be cut off as well.

"I promise not to crow again. Let me show you the white mice before you leave," said the cock, strutting along the path.

The white mice lived in a tiny house, painted green, with a wheel attached which revolved rapidly.

Here the mouse and his wife enjoyed every convenience for living, as they said themselves; in the wheel they could run round and round, without ever getting any further, when they needed exercise. Then they had a parlor and chamber above, with a window under the roof.

Tiny felt extremely queer when he saw the mice. All the cat nature within his small body asserted itself, and he felt a strong desire to pick their dainty bones at once, when nothing more than their pink noses were visible, peeping out of the door suspiciously.

"That is a cat," cried Madame Mouse, her nose growing pinker with excitement, and she immediately retired up stairs.

The kitten's eyes grew large, his whiskers twitched nervously, and in a moment the mouse mansion was overturned with a crash. The inmates ran out upon the grass, wicked Tiny in close pursuit.

"See what you have done," said the parrot, "with your politeness to strangers!"

The children to whom the pet mice belonged, came running out to rescue their favorites, if possible, from the enemy, just as Madame Mouse squeezed herself behind a stone, and Tiny pounced upon the other.

Alas, the children could not save him from the kitten : one shake of the cruel claw, and the poor mouse lay dead! The children placed him in a sugar-plum box, with flowers painted on the lid, wrapped in pink cotton from mamma's jewel-case, and dug a little grave, in which the remains were placed, with a bit of slate for a headstone.

The oldest boy, who went to school, wrote :

"Here lies my white mouse. He was killed by the cat, July 5th, 1868.

The others considered this very well done.

Tiny sat on the fence licking his paws, and looking down upon the funeral ceremonies with perfect unconcern. The kitten was not at all sorry or ashamed ; he only regretted that Madame Mouse was coaxed back into her house before he had the pleasure of eating her up.

It would have melted any heart, but that of a cat, to see the little widow mouse weeping over the loss of her mate.

The spaniel came bounding out, his silky ears pricked up to know what had happened.

" Bow, wow !" barked the dog. " What is going on ?"

"'The cat has eaten the mouse," croaked the parrot. " It is all the cock's fault."

Tiny curved up his back and spit at the spaniel, while the latter worried the kitten, although no further harm was done.

"A cat is never to be trusted," observed the spaniel.

Tiny was rescued at last by his mistress, and carried into the house in safety.

"I have learned a great deal," thought the kitten, curling himself into a ball upon the sofa for a nap, and then the Maltese fell asleep.

JACK'S CIRCUS.

NCLE WILLIAM had returned home from his long voyage to China, and all the children greeted his arrival with delight, for he told them famous stories, and brought them wonderful idols in gilt shrines, paper umbrellas that resembled toadstools when outspread, carved boxes of fragrant wood, and rose-tinted shells from the depths of the Indian Ocean. Jack was the eldest boy of the little flock, and it was his delight to follow the sailor about from place to place, asking a thousand eager questions about the sea; for Jack intended to become a sailor himself some fine day, and Uncle William had promised that he should sail in his ship—they had arranged the whole matter between them.

Several weeks passed away pleasantly. Uncle William strolled about, meeting old friends in church, at the post-office, and visiting such spots in the surrounding country as he used to ramble in when a boy. He also was invited out to tea-parties by careful housewives, and to pic-nics by the younger portion of the community. After this space of time he began to grow restless, pacing the piazza as though it was a quarter-deck, and smoking his pipe : the quiet monotony of country life wearied him. He longed for the fresh sea-breeze to fill out the sails of his vessel once more, and bear him swiftly away to other lands.

"I must be off to the city to-morrow," he said, rising from the supper-table one evening ; "the 'Sea-Gull' will take a cargo from New York to Liverpool, this time. What do you say to my carrying this little man with me to town, eh ?"

Jack's round face grew radiant at the idea, he cut a caper expressive of delight, and began to beat an imaginary drum upon his knees. Jack had never been to the city in his life ; but then he had visited the country town, and seen the court-house and jail, which is certainly the next best thing. All the other children regarded him as a hero, with envy and admiration, as he began to sort his choice valuables, selecting such of them as he should require on the projected journey. A new pop-gun, the "Second Reader" at school, if he felt literary at any time, and a few marbles, must accompany him on his travels. Uncle William interfered, allowing Jack only a small bag for his wardrobe, but the latter did carry the marbles in his pocket, secretly, the whole way, for what boy was ever happy without them?

The sun rose clear and bright, glistening over the trees just changing in Autumn's hues from green to vivid scarlet and yellow, when Jack started on his journey, the fresh morning air, with a frosty keenness in its breath, making his plump cheeks blooming as roses. How proud he felt when they drove to the railway-station, and he sauntered about on the platform swinging his bag, and fingering the marbles furtively in his pocket, while Uncle William bought the tickets, through a pigeon-hole, of an old gentleman in spectacles! A distant prolonged whistle, echoing among the hills, made Jack's heart bound: the train came smoothly gliding along the track, the locomotive discharging a cloud of steam with a loud shriek; then stopped abruptly, so that all the cars were thrown back with a wrenching jerk. Soon Jack was seated, the engine gave another puff, and away they started, towns, rivers, and forest whizzing past the windows in apparently endless succession.

Never did our hero's bright eyes have so much work to do, as he was not such a very aged person yet—only twelve years old! There was a fat old black nurse opposite, holding a tiny dog, wearing a collar fringed with silver bells; and beyond her sat a wonderfully pretty little girl, with soft hair like waving floss-silk, rippling down over her shoulders from beneath a velvet hat. The little lady looked like some beautiful tropical bird in glittering dainty plumage, and she seemed very proud of her small kid gloves. Beyond sat a young lady with a red nose, and a book in her hand, her head done up in a brown barege veil; and beyond her still, an old gentleman, whose double chins Jack counted with great interest—one, two, three, and so on down the line of passengers to the door. There was every kind of shaped head, and a great variety of faces, some dark and cross-looking, others frank and smiling. The conductor seemed a very important personage, and wore a fine diamond ring upon his finger: but then conductors are always expected to do that.

A droll shrewd-looking boy brought ice-water through the car, and Jack soon became very much interested in him—so much so, that he always took a glass of the water, as that enabled him to exchange a remark or two with the larger boy, who usually winked, and replied in slang terms which Jack did not in the least understand.

The boy must have kept a perfect storehouse in one of the baggage-cars, else he would not have been able to produce so many different articles which he offered for sale—magazines, newspapers filled with funny pictures, dreadful candies, gum-drops, and stale gingerbread.

Presently Jack's eyes closed in the most unexpected manner, and they did not open again until the car was in the tunnel, where it was so fearfully dark, and the bells on the horses tinkled dismally as they plodded along.

Now for the first time the country boy saw the broad streets of handsome houses; throngs of eager people hurrying past, each intent upon his own interests in life, and carrying a little world within himself of which the others knew nothing; and beautiful carriages with prancing horses, all flashing steel or gilt trappings, driven by grand coachmen in fine livery. He would have paused at every confectioner's window, where pink angels hovered about white sugar-castles, or sleek candy-oxen drew carts laden with delicious sugar-plums, and candied fruits, transparent crimson and golden balls; stopped to admire the skill of the little Italian harp-boys, whose brown fingers strummed some popular air; or to stare at a fantastic man in Turkish dress and turban, who advertised patent medicines in letters upon his back, had not Uncle William hurried him to the hotel where they were to stay.

Jack only remained two whole days in the city; but if we were to attempt describing all that he did, even in that short space of time, we should never get to the real object of our story—what he did when he arrived home once more. Uncle William took him to the circus in the afternoon, where horses dashed about with riders all gauze and tinsel, so that their garments seemed to be composed of splendid golden scales and precious jewels, to Jack's unaccustomed eyes ; and the clown cracked such merry jokes, seeming to look at Jack particular'y, when he said anything funny, which certainly was delightful.   Then followed all manner of athletic feats, in which a certain comical little boy, dressed like a miniature clown, climbed poles, leaped through hoops, danced on the tight-rope, and performed a hundred marvellous feats like a veritable monkey.

Nor was this all, a company of children performed the charming play of "Cinderella," and the whole affair was as natural as possible to Jack's mind.   The Prince drove the loveliest cream-colored ponies, just suited to a prince ; the two sisters were haughty, and snubbed Cinderella, while they admired their rich dresses in the mirror before going to the ball ; and the old godmother altered her godchild's rags with a wave of her wand, although she was observed to unfasten a string or so previous to the magical change.   When the glass slipper was finally placed upon Cinderella's foot, the whole affair concluded with feasting and music— little Court gentlemen in knee-breeches and cocked hats dancing with little Court ladies in satin trains and feathers.

Never had Jack imagined anything half so beautiful, and when he went to bed that night in the hotel, which smelt of soup everywhere, he dreamed he was the prince driving the pretty ponies, or the wicked elder sister, trying to force on the slipper. then he was the little clown, bounding about fearlessly through loops of rope and over bars, while the audience applauded his daring movements. They were really wonderful feats for a small boy, for at one moment he seemed to stand firmly upon a slender pole, and the next jumped through the air to catch a dangling rope, with a rush that made him awake, and start up to find Uncle William peacefully snoring in the opposite bed, and the morning sun peeping brightly through the curtains of the window.

Jack also went to visit the caged animals, lions, tigers, and bears, pacing the narrow limits of their prison-houses restlessly, or crouching upon the floor of their dens in repose. Jack gazed at their handsome striped fur, their huge paws, and sharp strong teeth, thinking of all the terrible stories he had read of them when roaming at large in forest and jungle; while the tigers glared at him savagely through the bars. the lurid green light in their eyes seeming to say—

"You would be a dainty morsel, young gentleman! If we had you in here, *wouldn't* we pick your bones!"

The glass aquariums were no less interesting. It seemed to Uncle William as though Jack would never tire of watching the pretty fish flash about through the clear water, or the brilliantly colored marine worms and crabs roaming among the sea-weeds and rocks at the bottom of this miniature ocean-world. The inhabitants of the aquarium fought, and struggled, and even ate each other up, they all felt so much at their ease in this adopted home ; but the crabs were especially amusing as they scrambled and sidled about in search of adventure, bold and prompt in every movement.

All things come to an end, it is said, and so Jack's visit to town terminated, and he returned home again, his little head crowded to overflowing with new ideas, for he had used his eyes and his eager tongue to the best possible advantage during the journey, wanting to know why *this* thing was done so and so, or why *that* one could not have been differently arranged, after the manner of all bright boys, until Uncle William was glad to deposit him safely in his country home once more.

Two long eventful days had passed since he had seen the quiet village street, with the neat houses framed in trees—the stretch of common where the cows loitered at night, on the road home, for a last mouthful of tender grass—and the comfortable farm-house further up, snugly stowed away at the base of a steep hill, which shielded it from the keen north wind in winter. Jack had crowded so much enjoyment into this brief space of time, that fancied he had been away for months inst days, and expected to find that the baby had grown an inch, the rosebush bloomed, and the white hen hatched a brood of chickens during his absence. He felt quite angry when he met boys from school, who accosted him with—

"Back already, Jack?" or, "Seems to me you didn't stay long."

The drollest part of all, however, was that he found himself telling his brothers and sisters about events which transpired a week before he left home. Jack became a hero in the family circle, the little flock of wondering listeners collecting about him on all occasions to hear his adventures told afresh. Jack's brain was clearly upset by the change in his hitherto quiet life ; he could do nothing in school but draw rows of houses on his slate—only they *would* not stand straight as the city houses really did ; and wonderful carriages drawn by wooden-looking horses, whose legs could not have been any manner of use to them, they were so stiff.

At length he devised a delightful plan : he would arrange a theatre for himself in the attic, on the next Saturday afternoon. The attic was a famous place, sloping away under the eaves into dark corners, where one half expected that some hobgoblin was hiding, to pounce upon any person who dared to venture near.

All manner of useless lumber was stowed away in odd nooks—fishing-rods, rat-traps, old hats without crowns, long-tailed coats ornamented with brass buttons, and portly rag-bags awaiting the arrival of the peddler, who would exchange them for bright tin pans and kettles. The sun darted golden beams through the narrow window down upon the carefully spread herbs, placed there by grandmother to dry—catnip, spearmint, and boneset, for winter use; and the spinning-wheel beyond, that no one used now, although Katy Brannick, the Irish girl, declared it hummed swiftly at night, guided by ghostly fingers,—but then it was only the wind in the chimney after all.

Jack told Richard Blake, the shoemaker's son, and his most intimate friend, all about his plan of giving an entertainment in the attic, and Richard entered into the project very heartily, although he did not quite understand what was expected of him, as he had not been to the city to learn.

All through the week the two boys were making mysterious journeys to the garret, and whispering together behind the door, until the other children began to wonder what secret was hidden away up stairs. There was nothing to be seen, however, when they peeped into the garret, except a few newspapers and ropes.

"Now, girls," said Jack, when the important day arrived, to his sisters Mary and Nanny, "I shall have a theatre in the garret this afternoon, and you may come if you wish, only you must do what we tell you, mind."

"We will, assented Mary and Nanny, quite delighted at the idea. "Can we bring Charlie, too?"

"Yes," replied Jack, running away at full speed to deliver some other invitations.

Saturday was always a very busy day at the farm. Mother had the large ovens heated to bake all varieties of tempting spiced cakes, crisp pies, and a delicious pudding; while it was consi'――d a great honor by the two little daughters if the; were allowed to prepare raisins (never eating one, of course), or beat eggs to a foamy lightness on such occasions, when a pleasant odor steamed through the broad kitchen, suggestive of the feast to come.

The good mother had no idea of the performance up stairs, to which she was not invited, for Jack dreaded being laughed at by the older people; she only realized that the children were quiet somewhere, and a moment of rest was a blessing to her.

A large bedquilt served to curtain off a portion of the attic, and the audience were requested to seat themselves quietly, after paying for admission a large pin upon entering, to Richard the doorkeeper. When they were arranged, Richard went behind the curtain to assist in the performance. The curtain should have been drawn aside quickly, but it caught on the string, and the whole affair tumbled down with a jerk, exposing the stage to full view, where Jack stood in one of his father's coats reaching to the ground, holding the carriage-whip in his hand.

Some of the audience were so impolite as to laugh when the curtain fell down.

"Never mind!" said Jack, cheerfully; "I am the ring-master, when I crack my whip the horses will go round in a circle."

Out came the riders in brave array, headed by the valiant Richard, three of them mounted on canes, and the fourth with an old umbrella for a charger. Then they pranced round the ring, Jack cracking his long whip to make them trot faster, and telling funny stories as he did so, only they did not sound one half so funny as they ought to have done, somehow.

The first scene was certainly a success, and the audience so much admired the cantering of the hobby-horses, that they began to skip about themselves, making a great deal of noise. Little Charlie, a sturdy rosy-cheeked boy of four years old, had remained very still at first, sitting between Mary and Nanny, staring about him with round blue eyes; but now he too became unruly, and insisted upon using his small legs, clad in red stockings of grandma's knitting, with the others. Shouts of merry laughter echoed through the old attic, even the more properly behaved little girls dancing about, when Charlie boldly seized one of the canes in his chubby fists and began to amble about the stage.

All this time Jack had been busily engaged dressing Richard as an old woman, in a long gown, apron, and poke bonnet.

"You must all shut your eyes till I tell you to look, as there is no curtain," shouted Jack.

Richard peeped out his head in the poke bonnet behind the beam, and whispered—

"I have forgotten what I was to say."

"Come along," whispered Jack in return, "and speak whatever comes into your head."

The children looked at Richard in silence, when they were told they could open their eyes, standing there in the poke bonnet, shaped very much like a coal-scuttle ; and Charlie stepping forward walked solemnly round the comical figure, not knowing who it was.

Richard was seized with stage fright ; he tittered foolishly enough, but seeing Jack Cook very angry, began to recite slowly—

"Twinkle, twinkle, little star."

When he had got through with one verse, he fled from the scene, tripping over his long dress ; and to the audience this seemed quite right, as a part of the play ; but poor Richard felt dreadfully sheepish over his failure.

Jack now brought out three large hoops covered with newspaper, and ornamented with painted devices, which had cost the boys great labor during the whole week.

"The man jumped through these hoops, and landed on the horse's back each time," said Jack. "I should make Wag be my horse to run under the hoops, but he growls and won't mind."

Wag was the huge Newfoundland dog, accustomed to romping with the children; still, he would not behave like a circus-horse, and even snapped at Jack when he tried to train him properly. Wag was contented to be an honest doggy, and nothing more.

The three hoops were placed in a row, supported on each side, and Jack sprang through the first one in gallant style, rending the paper just as the circus rider had done. The second one was cleared also, but in dashing through the third, Jack stumbled over Charlie, who was in the way as usual, and up tripped the little scarlet stockings, and down came the poor little head with a bump.

"Oh dear! he'll spoil all the fun if he cries," exclaimed Jack, pausing in his career for a moment.

Cry! Charlie understood that very well indeed, you may be sure. You sho uld only have seen him hold his breath until he was almost black in the face, and one expected his small body would almost explode; then give *such* a shout that every one jumped. The children tried to soothe him, but in vain, the bump on his head was too cruel to be speedily forgotten, until the little man was coaxed to step through the hoop himself, which cured his wounded feelings at once, and he began to laugh with the tears still fringing his eyelashes.

The fun that those hoops afforded !—even after the paper had been torn to fringes—for the others must jump through also, and it was surprising how soon they all learned to do exactly what Jack had done—except the girls, of course, they did not join in the romp.

"I am a bear now," said Jack, crawling forth on his hands and knees, with a buffalo skin on his back to look shaggy and terrible. "Richard is my keeper, and makes me behave because he beats me. I have not been fed all day, and that makes me ever so fierce—I shall eat up somebody quick."

The bear came mowling among the spectators, growling fearfully, and they fled screaming and laughing in various directions before the approaching monster. Richard forgot that he was to be keeper, and turned into a bear also, increasing the confusion and struggling among the merry crowd by his movements. Presently Charlie became quite savage too, and insisted on making himself into a small bear, which he did with such success, prowling about and pretending to eat up his sisters with those sharp little teeth like a squirrel's, that Jack rose up thinking they had growled enough, for a time at all events.

But sturdy Charlie had not been a bear long enough; he still went growling about, making the children laugh, and finally retired to a den behind the spinning-wheel, which he managed to knock over, breaking the spindle with a snap. What a deal of mischief little feet can do, especially when they belong to a boy of four years old who has become a *bear !*

Jack and Richard now began to arrange a tight-rope out of the clothes-line, hung between two beams : then the former put on a pair of slippers, and climbed upon the slender cord.

"What are you going to do ?" inquired the wondering audience.

"Walk on the rope," replied Jack.

"You will break your neck, Jack, I am sure," cried Nanny, anxiously.

"Nonsense !" said Jack ; "it can be done quite easily, if one keeps cool."

So he stood up on the rope, feeling very queer and giddy ; still he took two steps forward boldly—slipped, and sat down on the rope rather suddenly.

"I must have a balancing-pole, that is what I need," he said, bravely.

Poor Jack ! he could not do half so well as he had expected, it looked so easy to trip about on the tight-rope. With a broomstick for a pole he mounted up again, and such extraordinary capers as he cut—swaying sideways, stumbling forward, losing his balance and slipping to the floor, then scrambling back once more! It is only a wonder he did not come to grief sooner, although that happened speedily enough.

" I wear white-silk stockings and a velvet jacket all gold fringe, only you must imagine that part," said Jack, and just then the rope broke under him, so that he plunged headlong among grandmother's bundles of herbs, and against an old-fashioned looking-glass, which shivered into fragments.

At this moment the garret door opened, and Uncle William's sunburned face appeared on the stairs, followed by grandmother's cap and keen spectacles, freshly polished to discover anything amiss.

There sat Jack, a hero no longer, in the midst of a shower of glass, with his hands bruised and a cut upon his cheek, and when he beheld grandmother's severe nose, he began to cry.

Uncle William laughed, as he removed his pipe to puff out a cloud of smoke.

" What are you trying to do, you young monkey ?" he inquired, picking Jack up.

" What he saw in the city," piped Richard.

Uncle William chuckled again, and this made Jack's tears flow afresh.

" He has broken the clothes-line with his pranks," said grandmother, gathering up the pieces. " Dear! dear! how they have trained into my herbs!"

The children all trooped down stairs silently, **and Jack** was sent to bed as a punishment, when **his** wounds had been dressed ; but they were not one half so disagreeable as the disgrace of assuming one's night-clothes and creeping between the sheets while the sun was still shining.

After supper Nanny stole into the room softly, **to** give Jack her cake. He had been forced to swallow some of grandmother's herb-tea, which she gave for every ailment, although the hungry boy would much rather have received bread and butter instead. Later, Uncle William came up stairs to make a visit, when the sun had sunk in crimson glory below the horizon and Jack's little room was growing dark in the twilight.

"This will be a lesson to you, my boy," he said ; "you will leave the tight-rope dancing to the people trained for it. I don't believe you will ever have a theatre again, Jack."

"No, sir, I never shall," replied Jack, dismally And he never did.

How the Canary-bird Caught Cold.

OW we are to hear a sad history, but one that is quite true, nevertheless.

The canary was not to blame, it was all the carelessness of nurse in leaving him exposed on Christmas Eve, when the weather was extremely severe.

The canary usually resided in the conservatory, where the sun sparkled through the window-panes upon the japonica-trees studded with waxen crimson flowers, moss-baskets fringed with trailing vines, fragrant heliotrope, and geraniums with pink velvety blossoms. Here the canary trilled a little song to the flowers, flirted the seeds about his cage, and took a bath in the tub of water, for the pleasure of pruning out his dainty feathers afterward.

Two Java sparrows occupied another cage, and

the three birds were excellent friends : the sparrows admired the canary's voice, and the canary, in return, said that their white cravats and pink beaks were very pretty.

The gold-fish lived in a crystal globe below, but they were stupid, contenting themselves with displaying their brilliant scales and goggle eyes through the glass walls of their house, and seldom made any remark.

The gardener never allowed the conservatory to grow chill. the plants must have a warm atmosphere to perfume with their sweet presence ; so if the canary had been left there he would never have taken cold. Still, poor Dicky was not consulted in the matter.

"To-morrow will be Christmas Day," said one of the Java sparrows.   "Only see the snow fall outside !"

Nurse came in, took down the canary's cage, and carried it up stairs into the nursery, where one of the children lay upon the sofa, wrapped in one of his mother's flannel dressing-gowns, and taking horrible medicine every now and then.

Dicky was hung in the window, and as the sun shone brightly there, he soon felt quite comfortably at home and began to sing, first chirping briskly for a while, until his tiny throat expanded in a flood of melody, to the great delight of the sick child.

Dicky spent a very pleasant day.   He was treated to a lump of sugar, and then he sang louder by way of expressing his thanks ; yet when night came on, nurse forgot to return the bird to the warm conservatory,—she had so much to do in getting the children safely to bed, for they were half wild over the idea of Christmas presents, which would surely come on the morrow.

The gaslight flashed so brightly in Dicky's eyes that he could not close them and pop his little head under one wing, as he was in the habit of doing down stairs in the dark.

It was Christmas Eve, and the bird soon became interested in watching the older members of the family step softly about, unfolding mysterious parcels, suspending stockings filled with sugar-plums, and whispering in corners for fear of awakening the children, who were dreaming of Santa-Claus, clattering about on the roofs in fur boots and mittens, loaded with gifts for them.

Upon the table was placed a doll, dressed like a bride, in rich satin and orange blossoms, dainty white slippers upon her feet, and pearl ear-rings in her ears.

Beside her stood a funny negro, ready to dance when the board on which he was placed was tapped with the finger. A jumping-jack lay on his back staring straight up at the canary-bird, and Dicky felt positively sure that he winked drolly once or twice.

When the family retired the toys commenced to move and talk together pleasantly.

"I am made of the best kid," said the bride, spreading out her dress, and fanning herself gracefully with a tiny ivory fan she held in one hand.

"It is not so much what one is made of, as what one can do," replied the negro Jim Crow, dancing on the board, and keeping such excellent time that the bride even nodded approval, although such a "break-down" would not be allowed in the best society, she said.

As for the jumping-jack, he sprang up and began to skip about without the string being pulled which made him throw up his pasteboard arms in a jerky fashion.

A party of china dolls sat around a tea-table, which was spread with every dainty that a doll could desire—cups and saucers, a tea-urn, fruit and cakes, of painted wood.

They giggled together over the jumping-jack's idea of graceful steps; but then they were young and foolish.

"Do better if you can," cried the Jack, very angry.

The china dolls left the table and joined hands in a circle; still, they could not begin without fine music, so one of the number went to the little piano, but she did not know how to play very well, and therefore she declared the piano was badly out of tune.

The music-box on the mantelpiece came to the

?

rescue, and struck up a lively air, the sweet silvery notes tinkling out so prettily and distinctly that they sounded like drops of water splashing into a marble basin. The canary-bird was enchanted, for he had an ear to appreciate the melody.

Oh, it was a charming sight to see the china dolls dance, tripping about lightly upon their little china feet, forming circles, the bright dresses mingling together, then separating again, until the jumping-jack forgot his ill-humor entirely, and leaped up into the air so high that he would have broken his neck had he been anything else but a harlequin.

The whip-top could not keep still, so it twirled about in the waltz by itself; the ball bounced into the bride-doll's face, crumpling her delicate lace veil, then rebounded into the midst of the china dollies, toppling the little dancers over in confusion.

There never was such a clumsy ball !

While the dancers were gathering themselves up, very much tumbled by the fall, the lid of a box opened, and a stranger-doll rose up inside.

"I can walk," said the stranger-doll, proudly. "Be so good as to make way for me."

All the other toys drew back silently, leaving a clear space on the table, and the walking-doll skipped out.

Tramp, tramp, she marched across the table, her brass boots showing to great advantage beneath her short dress.

"Very well done for a machine," said a monkey on a stick.

The walking-doll paused to look at the monkey indignantly, and something clicked within her, so that she stood with one foot upraised, unable to move—the machinery had run down.

"Allow me to assist you," said the nimble jumping-jack, and offered his arm with all the grace of a Frenchman.

"I could walk if I chose to," said the doll; still, she climbed into her box again, and pretended to fall asleep, because she was so angry at the remarks of the impertinent monkey, and that her machinery had failed—after her boasting about it, too.

"Who needs medicine?" said the apothecary, standing behind the counter of his shop, where the drawers were labelled, bottles were ranged about, and a miniature pair of scales stood ready for use.

"The walking-doll would like something to mend her wounded feelings," said the monkey, with a grimace; and the remark was considered very witty by all the company, especially the merry-hearted china dolls, that laughed until the tea-cups rattled on the table.

"A plaster?" suggested the apothecary, nodding his head sagely.

"Nothing of the sort," snapped the walking-doll, from her box.

"Oh, I thought you were asleep," observed the monkey.

The apothecary-shop afforded a great deal of amusement, for toys like to play quite as well as children, it seems.

A little woolly dog on wheels rolled up to the counter and desired a cough mixture; he had barked himself very hoarse.

The druggist speedily prepared a certain cure, pouring mixtures from one bottle to another, with a wise air, sprinkling some powder out of a drawer, then charging a good round price for the trouble.

"That is too much," barked the dog.

"Drugs are high," replied the druggist; and he had the best of it, for the customer paid two crooked pins and departed.

Now a splendid tin coach, painted yellow, with prancing spirited horses came driving along the table, drawing up before the shop in grand style, while one of the tin footmen jumped down to open the door, that the lady might alight.

She was extremely elegant, sniffing daintily at the perfumes. Still, she emptied a long purse, and the footman was loaded with scent-bags, hair-brushes, and soap when she returned to the carriage; and the coachman cracked his whip smartly to drive back where they had been originally placed beside a book of games, near the wall.

Next a steamboat tinkled its bell, and darted
toward the shop swiftly, all the passengers standing
on the deck, with a flag waving above their heads.
The steamboat slid along on wheels, and did not
require water to move the paddles. The captain
was very gruff (although not an inch long and
made of wood.) as a captain should be, and gave
his orders through a trumpet.

The passengers ran down a ladder, one after another, and desired some remedy for sea-sickness. So
the druggist pounded in his mortar until he had
prepared pills enough to kill the whole of them ;
and with these they climbed upon the deck again
well satisfied.

Finally an elephant made of cotton-flannel, stuffed
with bran and carrying a houdah upon his back,
stepped slowly up to the door. The man seated in
the houdah, with a yellow turban upon his head,
was too dignified to visit a shop in person ; the
servant who held the peacock plume for a parasol
must do that, and none but the best spices could be
purchased either.

Each of the china dolls had some ailment : this
one suffered from headache or toothache, that one
had a pain in her little finger. It was surprising their
cheeks could remain so red when they really were
invalids.

So the toys came and went, while the canary-
bird drowsily watched their frolics ; and the strange,

part of it was, that no sooner did they pass over
the threshold of the shop than their packages vanished.

Dicky nodded wearily, dozed, and nearly tumbled from the perch : then he felt dreadfully cold.

The fire had died out, the storm dashed in flakes
of hail against the houses, the wind howled through
the deserted streets, drifting fine snow into cracks to
chill poor Dicky.

It was a fearful night: the rivers froze into a
crystal mirror from shore to shore ; the country was
wrapped in a crisp white robe, fringed with diamonds of powdered ice, and the thermometer sank
down, down to the nipping region of zero.

Dicky might have frozen stiff ; as it was, a mere
spark of life was left in his tiny body, when the servant came to kindle the fire in the early morning,
just as the children began to shout merrily over their
presents, taking such as they could back to bed, or
trotting in to show mamma what Santa-Claus had
brought to them.

When it was discovered what Dicky must have
suffered from the cold, the bird was caressed in
soft warm hands, and offered tempting seeds which
he could only peck at feebly.

Nor was this all, the children forgot their new
playthings to crowd around and watch the process
of dipping Dicky's feet into tepid water, and a drop
of brandy poured down his throat, which made him

very tipsy at the time, but really did no good afterward.

The cage was restored to the conservatory, and the Java sparrows welcomed the canary back cordially, wishing to know what he had seen during the long absence up stairs. So Dicky told them how the dolls danced on Christmas Eve, although he could only speak in quick fluttering breaths.

Winter passed along; the canary drooped more and more, he certainly seemed to be going into consumption, while no glad songs ever trilled out on the air from the formerly gay songster.

"Can nothing be done?" inquired the Java sparrows.

"Yes, certainly," replied the flowers. "The beautiful balmy Spring cures all diseases. Keep up your courage for a while longer, little mate."

Every morning the children peeped in to see if the birdie was better. If he died they promised to give a splendid funeral.

At length grandmother came, with her spectacles on. She was a famous bird-doctor in her way, and immediately ordered some olive-oil administered, and a trifle of madeira afterward, just to keep up his strength.

All at once Dicky began to improve. He spread his golden wings in the sunlight, and skipped from perch to perch as he had not done before for months. The snow had long since disappeared.

the trees in the city parks bloomed with tender green foliage once more, and through the half-opened windows of the conservatory a soft breeze rustled, telling of laughing brooks babbling along beside sloping banks of wild-flowers, and deep woods already animated by the music of birds.

Once more the canary's song rose gladly, in soft lisping trills and wonderful quavers, to the delight of the amiable Java sparrows.

"It is the coming of the Spring," rustled the flowers, expanding into greater beauty each hour. "We told you so."

Grandmother declared it was the olive-oil, and nothing else.